MW01100506

Winner of the 29th Annual
International 3-Day Novel Contest

Cooper,
wicked name — hope you
enjoy the books!

The Convictions of Leonard McKinley

Brendan McLeod

3-Day Books
Vancouver, Toronto

The Convictions of Leonard McKinley
Copyright © 2007 by Brendan McLeod

All rights reserved. No part of this book may be reproduced by
any means without the prior permission of the publisher, with the
exception of brief passages in reviews.

Edited by Derek Fairbridge
Designed by Trevor Boytinck, www.hatchcreative.ca
Cover images by Jeremy Bruneel

Library and Archives Canada Cataloguing in Publication

McLeod, Brendan
The Convictions of Leonard McKinley / Brendan McLeod.

ISBN 978-1-55152-222-7

I. Title.

PS8625.L45C66 2007   C813'.6   C2007-902835-7

Printed and bound in Canada by Hemlock Printers.
Printed on 40% post-consumer recycled paper.

Distributed in Canada by Jaguar and in the United States by
Consortium through Arsenal Pulp Press (www.arsenalpulp.com).

Published by:
3-Day Books
341 Water Street, Suite 200
Vancouver, B.C., V6B 1B8
Canada

www.3daynovel.com

For Nola, Sam and Kelly. Intrepid 3-Day companions who know love, saints and invasive medical procedures, which is really all you need.

And thanks, Lo, for letting us use your house.

Part One

WHEN LEONARD TURNS SIX, HIS FATHER buys him a bike without training wheels because he wants to learn to ride like he is escaping from assassins with lasers. Leonard's father shuffles him up and down the street, breathing hard at his side until he sustains heart palpitations and Leonard takes off on his own. He flies around the suburban streets of Calgary until he can no longer see his house and has to stop at a store for directions.

"I can't tell you unless you buy something," says the clerk. Leonard has no money, so he kicks down the newsstand outside and rides away crying. Two hours later a policeman finds him sulking against a tree and puts his bike into the backseat. He drives Leonard halfway home, but pulls a U-turn after hearing the whole story. They return to the convenience store and the policeman disappears inside for ten minutes. When he comes back out Leonard asks him what happened.

"I gave the bad man a ticket," says the officer.

"What for?"

"Being a dick."

"*Awesome*," says Leonard.

The policeman pulls away. "Did you kick down his newsstand?"

"Yes."

"Good."

When the policeman pulls up in front of Leonard's house his father is being wheeled away on a gurney. The large lights of an ambulance reflect off the gleam of the neighbours' gaping mouths behind their windows. Leonard's older brother Steve is standing on the walkway, his hands over his lips as though afraid something will escape from him.

Leonard's younger brother Nick is wandering around outside wearing the costume from his fourth birthday party last week. Their mother had allowed him to dress up as the sheriff, so he locked his friend Pete in the laundry room after he hadn't given him a present that involved the California Raisins.

Now, Nick moseys up to the police car. Leonard and the officer quickly get out.

"You killed Dad!" Nick shouts at Leonard. Then he shoots the police officer full of imaginary bullets and dives behind a bush.

"Shut up, Nick!" Steve yells.

Their mother runs up to Leonard and holds him tight to her waist. Then she smacks him on the bum for going missing and kisses his forehead to assure him their father is going to be okay.

Mrs. Shelbourne from next door comes over to look after them while their mother follows the ambulance to the hospital. They eat dinner in silence. Steve, who is in grade six, won't talk to Leonard because he is just a stupid little kid who still gets lost. Nick won't speak to Mrs. Shelbourne because she beat him at Hungry Hungry Hippos, except to briefly accuse her of cheating. Mrs. Shelbourne threatens to send him to his room for being impertinent, so Nick says he was just worried about their dad in the hopes that she'll feel sorry for him and give him a cookie. She doesn't fall for it and Nick refuses to eat his peas in protest.

Long after Leonard has gone to bed, he hears the garage door open underneath him. Footsteps fill the silence and his father's confident voice floats up the stairs as he explains to Mrs. Shelbourne that it was nothing more than a routine check-up.

"Perhaps a salad now and again," she chastises.

Leonard listens to Mrs. Shelbourne's departure and his parents' tread along the stairs. They check on the boys in succession and when they arrive at his room Leonard pretends to be asleep so it is one less thing they have to worry about.

When at last the sounds of his parents stop, Leonard lies awake wondering what had gone wrong. He prays that if his father eventually dies, he at least has a funeral with a closed casket, so everyone at school doesn't find out how fat he is. Leonard wishes his father were strong like the policeman from today, who encouraged him to kick over newsstands and called everyone he didn't like a dick.

AS PUNISHMENT FOR GOING MISSING, Leonard is confined to biking on Cedar Place for two weeks. He explores every inch of it, going so deep into the heart of its alleys that his parents have to put a bell on the porch to call him in to dinner.

Every night, Leonard finishes the day by racing himself to the lone lamppost at the far end of his street. He rushes towards it, the houses falling away on one side, and as he circles the body of his bike leans low and his tires whisper uneasily, skidding over the cement.

One night, Leonard tries to loop around the pole and smashes into it. His head flies through the handlebars framed the same way his Uncle Bruce hangs caribou from his cottage walls.

His father sympathizes but insists he get back on his bike right away. He tells Leonard that when he was sixteen and just learning to drive he took the car out to Waskesiu and on the way back got stuck shifting from neutral to first after a red light. An old man smashed into him from behind and swore at him for the three minutes it took to get the car back in gear and drive away. By the time he arrived home he never wanted to drive again.

"But my father got me back behind the wheel immediately," he says. "And now, for the rest of my life, I've been able to drive. It's an important skill. Like when the man came and took me away in the ambulance. See, that was important. *And,* if he had *also* suffered a heart attack, I'd have been able to fill in and drive us both to the hospital on time. *Eh*? That's why driving is the best!"

Leonard nods. His father walks down the drive with him and watches while he lines up his bike to the road.

"I *guarantee*," says his father. "You'll be fine. Pop-a-wheelies in no time."

His father watches Leonard take off. When his son is halfway down the street he stops clapping and takes his newspaper back inside. Leonard continues on, but at the end of the street he hits the post once more.

Back on the driveway, Leonard's father sees him call his bike a traitor and throw it across the lawn, nearly taking Captain's head off.

"*Hey*—watch the dog!" calls his father. "What's this all about?"

"You're a *liar*!" shouts Leonard.

Leonard's father sends him up to his bedroom to think about what he's just said. Leonard sits and hates his father, even though he feels guilty for almost killing Captain, who is the best dog in the universe because even though he's just a terrier he'll still take swipes at big dogs like Rottweilers, who are always on the news for eating old people and babies.

His mother knocks on his door twenty minutes later to explain how his father simply believes in the utility of exaggeration.

"He was just trying to get you to think positively," says Leonard's mother. "He doesn't mean you'll be performing actual pop-a-wheelies. It's like when he tells you that you're full of hot soup. That's not a lie. It's just funny. It's a joke, like when he tells you he had no girl-friends before Mommy. But of course he had. You get that, right?"

Leonard nods his head but in fact does not under-stand. Instead, he plans to assassinate his cheating father with a rifle as soon as he's old enough to buy one from the store.

After his mother leaves, Leonard stays in his room and imagines himself smashing into the lamppost again and again. That night, he falls asleep on impact and wakes up the next morning imagining the wreckage. He starts to tap twice every hour on the smallest parts of his body, the tip of his elbow and his pinkie toes, checking for breaks.

Two days later, Leonard hits the post again. He con-templates the idea that his street is cursed and asks Steve if the city will inspect it. Steve says he should write to Robert Stack, who wears the trench coat and is the lead investigator for *Unsolved Mysteries*, which is the scariest television show in the history of the world. The McKinley children are not allowed to watch it, though Steve has managed to tape a few episodes because their father just beats up on electronics and can't program the VCR. When they are alone downstairs Steve plays Leonard the tape, but the theme song scares him so much he pretends he has to go to the bathroom and never comes back.

Leonard knows that he will inevitably need his bike skills because he wants to become a spy, and so will often be caught in situations where he has to drive motorbikes across tightrope wires while carrying precious jewels just before a bridge blows up. So the next day he marches stoically through the garage, grabs his bike off the wall, and pedals bravely toward the tip of his driveway.

Leonard rides halfway down the street before he gets off his bike and walks it the remainder of the distance. He stops in the middle of the road, parallel to the lamppost, and tiptoes away from it to the opposite side of the street. He marches two feet forward and turns around.

For the fourth time, he hits his head on the post.

Leonard lies on the ground imagining meteors destroying planets and lost stars colliding in an enormous universe. He wants to touch every part of himself until he is completely protected from accidents.

He gets up and spits gravel down the sidewalk. At home, he announces that he will never ride his bike again. His mother asks how he keeps hurting himself and he tells her it's the weather.

＞ー＜

EVERY NIGHT, LEONARD'S FATHER eats vegetables and white pasta out of a box so that he doesn't have any more heart attacks.

"It's his special food," Leonard's mother says, patting him on the shoulder.

Leonard's father hates his special food. Whenever he puts the fork to his mouth he pretends he is going to die. All the boys look away and bite their lips because it is a strict McKinley rule to never take dinner for granted, and if they so much as titter their mother will stare at them so that their skin melts into their chairs.

"It's for your own good, Doug," says Leonard's mother.

"Moderation is going to kill me," says Leonard's father.

One night, while Leonard kneels at his bed to say his prayers, he hears a latch shut in the backyard. He tiptoes to the window and sees the tip of his father's cigarette glow cherry red behind a tree in front of the sandbox. Leonard gets so angry he returns to his bedside and prays with all of his might for God to rain lightning down on that tree and burn the top of his father's head off. He waits in silence, listening for a distant crackle that never comes, hearing only the latch of the gate open and close once more.

Later that year, Steve is lining up snowmen on either side of a dividing line in the backyard in order to re-create the historic battle of Waterloo. Leonard and Nick are spying on him from a dugout, waiting for him to put the finishing touches on his last soldier so that they can run out and destroy them before Steve has a chance to appreciate his work.

Leonard absently digs into the side of the hill with his glove and hits a buried bag. Knowing what he has found, he covers it quickly and pushes Nick out of their hole with an encouragement to get a head start on destruction. Their position blown, Nick springs into action and starts randomly tearing the heads off snowmen. Steve goes red to the wrists and chases Nick around with a hockey stick yelling about how he has no integrity.

In the dugout, Leonard unearths a plastic bag filled with chocolate and cigarettes. He hides it under his jacket, makes his way up to his room, and buries it in his closet under a stack of school binders from the year before. Leonard eats two chocolate bars every day after school for almost a month and his parents wonder why he has suddenly started acting up. When he runs out of candy, he buys more with the money he makes selling cigarettes for a quarter each to older kids at his elementary. He deals by the fence across from the soccer field and runs a thriving business, though at home, he hates his father for being fat and a liar.

"Humanity is capable of astounding accomplishments," Leonard's father tells the boys. "We've landed on the moon. Put robots on Mars. Invented the wheel!"

"The wheel was easy," says Nick.

"It might seem that way now because wheels are everywhere. They're ubiquitous. That means 'everywhere.' But imagine you had never seen a wheel. It's an extraordinary accomplishment."

"Yeah," says Steve.

"That's why you can grow up to do anything you want," says their father. "Look at me. They said I couldn't stop smoking. I'm not smoking. They said I wouldn't lose weight, and here I've lost forty pounds."

Leonard knows his father hasn't lost any weight at all because he continues to find bags of goodies hidden all over the house. With each successful piece of detective work Leonard's enthusiasm for the trade increases, until each day he is coming home from school to make a detailed search of the entire premises before his father comes home from his job as an accountant.

If a hunt is ever unsuccessful, Leonard closes his eyes and prays for God to guide him to a correct location. He knows this is good practice for his future life as a spy because Steve has told him about the Canadian Security Intelligence Service, which Leonard wants to work for as a religious secret agent. He will infiltrate enemy countries like Greenland and inspire a movie starring Michael J. Fox as a spy who relies on prayer to get himself out of difficult situations the way MacGyver uses chewing gum and popsicle sticks to escape from terrorists.

Leonard has reason for such optimism because his searches almost never fail. If they do, it is only on a day like the one where Nick punched the crap out of one of his hockey teammates after the boy said Leonard's father would be the perfect NHL goalie because all he has to do is stand in the net and block every shot without moving. Upon hearing this, Leonard's father, who had long since given up his special meals, skipped the red meat and reached across the table for the carrot sticks. Halfway through dinner, their mother leaned over and gently squeezed his wrist.

Yet things always return to normal. That summer, the family drives back from their cottage in Saskatchewan and when they stop in Hanna for ice cream their father eats right along with them. Their mother no longer even takes the time to frown.

Their father is fond of saying that gluttony is next to godliness, and heart attacks are good for shaking things up a bit. Their mother will smack his knee and tell him to shush, "you'll scare the neighbours." Leonard agrees because nothing is next to godliness because God can do anything, even bring down the sky.

Part Two

THE MORNING LEONARD IS TO BEGIN junior high, his mother wrests him from bed an hour early.

"I've made your breakfast," she tells him. "Come down when you've put on the clothes I bought you."

The week before, Leonard and his mother had gone shopping. For the first time in his life he was allowed to pick out brand-name t-shirts and shoes.

"Try those jeans," said his mother. "They should be baggy like that."

Leonard came home and paraded his new wardrobe back and forth in front of the television, flexing his muscles in front of everyone while Nick complained his life sucked because they hadn't gotten him anything.

"When you get to grade seven," their mother told Nick. Then she forced Leonard to get out of his clothes immediately and stop bragging or she would run them back to the mall quicker than you can say ungrateful.

"They're for school and school *only*," she called after him.

"Those look *terrible*," said their father. "It's 1992, not the future."

"Shush," said their mother. "Baggy is in style."

Steve said it didn't matter what was in style, the clothes were simply ludicrous and she shouldn't support Leonard bowing to the demagogue of commercialism.

"You obviously don't recall junior high," she replied. "You weren't always in grade twelve."

"How much did those clothes *cost*?" asked their father.

"Of all things," she said, "we can certainly afford a little peace."

After Leonard showers he dresses in a Quicksilver t-shirt and comes downstairs for his cereal. His mother tries to comb his hair while he eats, but he bats her away and tells her to leave him alone.

"I've bought you deodorant," she tells him, handing him a stick. "If you play basketball, wear it afterwards. The girls will appreciate it."

"I don't care," says Leonard.

"Well, you will."

"This smells."

"That's the point."

"It smells like French people."

Despite the shopping spree, Leonard is still angry with his mother because she has insisted on his commuting across the city to stick with his French Immersion program, when nearly all of his friends are dropping out and going to the neighbourhood English school.

"I'm going to be a *social pariah*," Leonard tells his mother. He knows this phrase from a sign on Steve's door: Proud to be a Social Pariah.

"Not if you smell nice."

Leonard has objected to his mother's decision because he wants to be a fireman, and won't need to speak French because all he'll have to do is save burning people from buildings and rescue cats.

"You could change your mind," says his mother.

"No," says Leonard. "I will definitely become a fireman."

"Well what if you wanted to become a fireman in Montreal?"

"I wouldn't go there because I don't speak French."

"Well you will."

"Mom!"

"What? Maybe one day you'll be saving someone in a fire and they'll be French and they won't be able to understand your directions in English."

"Then I'll just pick them up and haul them outside."

"Well what if you fall in love with a French girl?"

"No way! They smoke and play accordions!"

"I think you will fall in love with a French girl. A French girl named *Lizette*."

"Fine. But she'll smoke and then so will I. And then I'll die."

"Fine. Then you won't get to become a fireman."

Leonard has never won an argument with his mother because she was her high school valedictorian. In her speech she compared her classmates to boats leaving the harbour because she thought it was original. Their father says this is the only mistake she has ever made.

When Leonard is set to leave, his mother reminds him not to lose his brand new backpack and holds him tight for a moment.

"Don't be too sensitive," she says.

Leonard's mother always calls him her most sensitive child, even though last year he finished third out of every boy in grade six in a recess arm wrestling competition. She also calls him her handsome young man because of his dark brown eyes and delicate features, but only when they are alone, because otherwise Nick says he looks like a girl and Leonard has to give him a charley horse.

"Have lots of fun," says Leonard's mother, adjusting his coat.

"*Oui, oui,*" he replies.

When he reaches the bus stop Leonard stands alone, fixing his new crew cut and quietly judging everyone. Then he mentally lists his remaining friends and assesses them on a scale of one to ten, where ten stands for best friend and one for arch nemesis:

John: was cool and popular last year and had the nickname 'Juan' because he went to Spain for two weeks (big deal). Is not good at sports but is good at drawing, which is how he got to date Michelle for three days. Has a big head that could work against him, but people might not notice because he's so funny. Stay friends with him but make fun of his head if he's mean to you.

Friendship score: 8

Mark: really good at sports and has good hair. Might be using me for my trampoline. Not very funny, but stronger than me and better at hockey. So stay friends with him and invite him for sleepovers because I am the only person he will know who can play sports.

Friendship score: 6 (hope to move this to 9)

Amanda: is pretty and wears good make-up, usually. Super mean, but in grade five got kept after school with me by Mme. Bocquentin, who said we were pulling each other's hair because we were in love. Now she doesn't speak to me but she might in order to gang up against John, who she's feuding with since he used his power to have people start calling her "Santa Amanda" because of her deeper voice. Be nice to her at the beginning, for sure.

Friendship level: 5 (possible girlfriend, though)

Seleena: good friend. Don't want to kiss her though. All-time first girl to call my house.

Friendship level: 9

The only one of the four on the same route as Leonard is John, who arrives just in time for the bus. He is assigned to sit with a pretty girl with ribbons in her hair, while Leonard is seated next to a small boy named Ron who already has a moustache. They don't speak, and the bus begins its slow meander across town.

All the way to school, Leonard hears the pretty girl giggle at everything John says. He and Ron wince in tandem, so they might just become friends.

TWO WEEKS LATER LEONARD LEARNS that Darrell O'Reilly is dating Susan Orchester and letting other guys touch her breasts for five dollars. They meet in the exercise room after school at 3:35 p.m. in the nook behind the leg press. While the boys wait their turn they lift weights to burn off the excitement, and the football coach is impressed by their dedication. Darrell O'Reilly jogs on the spot, the change jingling in his pockets, steadily pacing towards a fortune.

He, Shel Nordstrom, Brent Campbell and Chris Eagles are all transfers from St. Lucy's Elementary, where they reputedly started a gang in the third grade whose mandate was to beat up redheads. They followed a boy named Richard home every day threatening to beat the freckles off his face until one afternoon his mother came out of the backyard with a water hose and told them her husband was a six-foot biker who would kick ass first and take names later. They didn't believe her, but, just in case, they switched to beating on smart kids, so if they ever asked you what the biosphere was or how precipitation formed you had to say you didn't know, or they would put you in the playground tunnel, each take an extremity, and quarter you until you promised never to study again.

Now they have gym glass together and they wait for Kyle McDonald to take off his shirt and change into his gym strip. Kyle is fat; his breasts sag over his belly like the naked picture of the old woman Chris Eagles had waited to pass around in shop class because the teacher is one year away from retirement and wouldn't hear the giggling. When Kyle takes off his shirt Darrell O'Reilly takes one of his arms and Brent Campbell takes the other, while Shel Nordstrom and Chris Eagles force all the other students into a chant urging Kyle to jiggle his tits.

Kyle wants to resist. Leonard sees the strain cause an indent across his brow like it was sliced with a box-cutter and his skin goes white like a scar. But Darrell O'Reilly and Brent Campbell have been touching Susan Orchester's breasts a lot as of late, so they are getting a lot of exercise, and they hold Kyle tight so the blood stops pumping past his wrists and his hands go numb. Leonard watches Kyle's eyes close for a moment and listens to the locker room scuttle into silence as Kyle bobs back and forth so that the fat on his chest ripples like a loose parachute in the wind. Darrell O'Reilly and Brent Campbell keep his arms up on either side in the position of the crucifix so that the rest of his body retains that same starting pose of near defiance while his chest leaps out and away from him like it was no longer his own. Shel Nordstrom and Chris Eagles insti-gate the laughter that soon swells until the students hear one another coming out of the walls, Leonard joining in on the din, and it continues like this until they let Kyle go.

Then all the boys finish dressing and go upstairs to play floor hockey. Darrell O'Reilly asks Kyle to borrow twenty-five cents for a pop, Kyle has to hand over a quarter, and Darrell O'Reilly claps him on the back with a friendly smack that will surely leave a mark.

›››‹‹‹

LEONARD IS ESPECIALLY UPSET with Darrell O'Reilly because he knows his brother Steve has faced similar attacks. When he was Leonard's age he once came home with a dent above his eyebrow after a classmate attacked him with a baking tray during Home Economics because Steve was a finalist in the spelling bee and knew how to spell words like dialysis.

That night at dinner, when Steve showed his parents the injury and explained that no disciplinary action had been taken, their father punished a chicken leg and their mother's eyebrows arched like they had just grown wings.

"Perhaps you should outline the event in writing," she suggested.

Emboldened, Steve retreated to his room after dinner and composed a voluminous letter to the authorities. While he was upstairs, their father and mother spoke in low tones over the running of the kitchen sink, though by the time Steve had finished his letter their father had returned to his usual self. He looked it over proudly.

"A scathing indictment! You write with such passion!"

The next morning, their mother drove Steve to school. Steve later told Leonard that though she never stopped smiling, she asked to speak to the principal with such force that the words cast the secretary's dress up past her knees. The principal came out kowtowing and Steve never saw the assailant again. Their father was fond of saying their mother forced him to move to Bermuda, "*Aloha*!"

Leonard now hopes for the same sort of support from his mother, but when he comes home she informs the boys of her plans to return to work.

"At a job?" asks Nick.

"Yes. A good job. At Foster Parents Plan, which is a charitable organization."

"We know Foster Parents, Mom," says Leonard.

Nick demands to know who is going to cook.

"Your father and I will split it."

Nick is immediately pacified. Every time their mother goes to visit family in Saskatchewan, their father either orders Chinese food or cooks steak and baked potatoes on the barbeque.

"*Bonne voyage*!" he exclaims, and hurries away with a stick in his hands.

But later that week their father has a late business meeting at the bank and leaves Leonard in charge of prepping dinner. His father arrives home well past eight o'clock capable of putting away a mutton chop, but Leonard looks at him over an unopened bag of pasta and asks him how to boil water. So their father reschedules the rest of the week in order to make them steaks every night and Nick eats three at every sitting and tells him he's the best cook in the world.

Right off the bat, Leonard's mother begins arriving home from work so late at night that all the children hear from her is the odd snap of her ankles like ball bearings on the dark stairs. Friday night is still set aside for family dinner, though the first night their mother comes home early she drags Nick inside and across the hallway floor bleeding out his nose onto the linoleum.

"Just take a look at your youngest son," she tells their father.

"What happened?"

Nick tells their father that George Henderson scored a clearly illegal goal after a glove pass in the offensive zone and when Nick told George that the goal should be disallowed George hacked at his leg with his stick. So Nick cross-checked him and George ran inside and brought out all three of his older brothers. Despite all of Nick's valiant efforts, he could only handle two of them before one got a good shot at his nose.

"I'm sure that's all true," says their father. "Now sit and eat your pork chops."

But their mother says that there will be no dinner for Nick tonight because not only do the McKinley children not believe in lying, they certainly don't believe in pre-historic behaviour and violence.

"But this is our one family dinner," says their father.

Sensing his chance, Nick says that he swears he's telling the truth and if he and Leonard and maybe even Steve aren't immediately allowed to march over there and put a hole through the Henderson's front window then the McKinley family will be the laughingstock of the neighbourhood and will have forfeited all self-respect. Even their father cringes at this, and Leonard actually sees the hair on the back of his mother's neck stand as she pushes Nick up the stairs.

The door to Nick's room slams and the remaining four eat the majority of their family dinner in silence, listening to Nick's livid footsteps battle the floor beneath him.

"He has to learn," says their mother.

Their father does not say anything because he recognized Nick's speech from one of the gangster movies they had all watched together while their mother was working late. Their father had rented it after Steve told him that Martin Scorsese was America's greatest contemporary filmmaker and Nick said he wanted to see something with lots of blood.

"I worry about his tendencies," continues their mother.

"I'm sure he didn't instigate it," says their father.

"Which is an overused excuse. And well beside the point."

"Maybe the same thing happened as two years ago," says Steve, referring to the time Nick had seen a cute girl coming toward him and picked up a rock and threw it in the air to impress her.

"And it landed on his head!" exclaims their father. The boys kill themselves laughing, so that their mother softens and allows Nick to come downstairs for dessert, provided he first finish the rest of his meal.

"I'm *starving*!" says Nick. "I was about to eat my Power Ranger!"

"What if toys *were* edible," Steve muses.

Steve wants to become either an artist or an inventor, and so one of his heroes is Dr. Yoshiro Nakamatsu from Japan, who holds over 2,500 patents and has written four doctoral theses. His invention process ends with his being submerged in a swimming pool and writing his thoughts out using an underwater pen, so Steve once argued that if their parents cared about his scientific future they would put a pool in the backyard.

"There's a shovel in the garage," their father had answered.

Back at the table, Nick says Steve should invent something worthwhile, like a machine that could turn hard chocolate chip cookies into soft ones, or hockey goalie pads that were attracted to rubber the same way magnets are attracted to metal.

"Then I could be a goalie in the NHL," says Nick.

"Oh, you'll get there on sheer perseverance," encourages their father. He looks over at Leonard. "Both of you, each to your particulars."

Leonard, like Nick, is an athlete, though he plays basketball, which is under funded in Canada. Thus far he has only been able to play in community leagues, where he scores with ease, though now that he is in junior high he is eligible to play school basketball, where the competition is much fiercer.

On Sunday when the family goes to church and the minister asks everyone to pray for whatever is in their heart, Leonard offers up a request to the Lord to allow him to make the school's basketball team, because he knows he is good enough and if he doesn't it will be a travesty of justice. He also prays for other people, like those who are poor and starving in Third World countries, but he reminds Jesus that he could do more for them as the most valuable player in the NBA than he could should something go wrong and he were inexplicably excluded from this year's Cypress Grove Lions junior boy's team. In fact, he makes a pact with God that should he ever make the NBA he will donate half his wealth to charities and do free endorsements for groups like the SPCA, which, he points out, is a better deal than God is going to get from a lot of other future basketball Hall of Famers.

Leonard knows that his prayers stand a good chance of succeeding because the featured passage of the day is Psalm 37, "*Trust in the Lord and do good...delight yourself in the Lord and He will give you the desires of your heart,*" which means that as long as you believe in God you can do anything you want. To illustrate this fact, his Sunday School teacher, Mrs. Rose, has him play a game in which all the students pair up and stand one in front of the other. On the count of three they are to lose their balance and let themselves fall backwards, trusting their partner to catch them in their arms.

But Leonard doesn't trust his partner because he is two years younger and skinny and probably can't hold him. So Leonard just bends back as far as he can and always keeps at least one half of both of his feet on the floor. When Mrs. Rose suggests he give in and trust his partner the same way he trusts God, Leonard thinks, *yeah, right,* it would be different if his partner actually was God because God is capable of all sorts of things, like creating the world in six days and listening to millions of people's prayers at exactly the same time and curing blind people whenever he feels like it, which is way more than this skinny guy could ever do.

"Lean *back*," says Mrs. Rose.

Leonard thinks that if he lets himself fall and the boy doesn't catch him he could sue the church the same way Jeremy Mayes took the school to court after he cut off his finger during shop class, and then his parents got rich and bought him a Sun Ice jacket. But at the same time Leonard realizes that the point of the exercise is that God has put his partner there and he should trust God to provide for him, and so he feels guilty for being a Doubting Thomas and thinking of suing the house of the Lord.

Leonard touches his body twice and leans back.

⋙⋘

ON THE DAY OF BASKETBALL TRY-OUTS, Leonard wakes up extra early to pray. He makes a deal with God that he will honour his father and mother for the rest of his life, regardless of whether he agrees with their decisions or not, just so long as the Lord ensures he makes the team.

So before leaving for school that day Leonard makes an early Mother's Day card and tucks it under his parents' bed sheets. Then he leaves a steak out to defrost and sets the television at the sports channel, so that his father won't have to lift a finger once he arrives home from work.

At school, he is nervous for the whole day, especially when every single student he talks to says they're also trying out for the team. Leonard eats lunch with Seleena, who tells him not to worry because he was the best basketball player in their gym class, but this is of little comfort because everyone thinks she has a crush on him. In French class Jill McMullen had blushed and handed him a note that asked what it was like to lick Paki pussy, even though the note could not have originated with her because she volunteered with handicaps and so would never have written something so mean. Ever since, Leonard has been ashamed to be seen in public with Seleena because he needs to look available to get a hot girlfriend. Plus, Seleena is only of medium popularity, while Leonard feels he is on the verge of joining the awesome crowd, especially if he makes the basketball team and his crossover dribble becomes the stuff of legend.

At basketball practice after school, the boys take the basketballs out of their steel racks and warm up by shooting dozens each to a hoop, so that whether or not a shot is successful depends more on random collision courses than any specific trajectory. When the coach arrives he blows his whistle twice and has everyone line up on the baseline, though there is not enough room and they pack in dozens deep.

"Never mind," says the coach. "Try five different lines."

This takes another ten minutes to sort out, and then the coach blows his whistle once more.

"Start running."

Everyone falls all over themselves, but it doesn't matter because the coach has gone out into the hallway. He comes back ten minutes later and blows his whistle again.

"Three-man weave."

Leonard promises God that if he performs well in the three-man weave he will open up an adoption agency when he is older that will care for neglected children. And Leonard is rewarded because he gets the opportunity to shoot the lay-up at the end of the exercise, which he sinks with grace. But the coach is gone again, and when he re-enters his whistle blows a final time.

"All right good work, guys. That's enough for today."

By the time the players have returned from the locker room there is a list of twelve boys outside the coach's door and his car is gone from the staff parking lot. Leonard stands on his toes above the flurry of heads. He promises that he is devoted to God in the same way that caused St. Lucy to pluck out her eyes after a suitor found them attractive in order to demonstrate that she only had love for the Lord.

And by the grace of God, Leonard finds his name on the sheet.

THAT NIGHT LEONARD'S FATHER IS ANGRY because somehow a steak was left out and bled all over the counter so that Captain licked it up and got sick on the carpet.

"I don't know how to get this stuff out," he calls from

his hands and knees, weighing a bottle of vinegar against a box of baking soda.

"You should mix them and see if they explode," says Nick.

"That sounds productive," says their father. "Who left the television on all day? Nick, were you watching highlights this morning?"

Nick says he wasn't. Their father rises from his knees and says he wishes Nick would just tell the truth for once because it was the sports channel that was left on and so it was obviously him. Nick gets mad and insists he's not lying, and even if he was who cares because he never complains when their father plays Elton John's stupid song "Rocket Man" on repeat.

"The best defence is a good offence," says their father, and tells Nick he can't watch the Flames game until the third period.

Nick slams his door so loud the windows rattle, but Leonard doesn't care about family strife because he's on the Cypress Grove basketball team.

That night Leonard prays to God to keep his streak going by having him succeed at the upcoming school dance. He promises God that if he gets to dance with Angela Watson he will never have pre-marital sex with her, or even be like John and show her off as his girlfriend by putting his hand in the ass pocket of her jeans while they walk down the hall together. To demonstrate his chastity, he agrees to date her for two weeks before he even tries to kiss her, so that their love will certainly be pure, like it is in Christian romance novels by Janette Oke.

Leonard lays in bed, enamoured of the Lord, feeling sorry for non-Christians who have to work out problems by themselves. He tells God that when he retires from the NBA he will become a faith healer and encourage heathens to give it all up to God, using today's basketball try-out as an example of personal development through faith.

AT THE END OF THEIR FIRST PRACTICE the basketball team is divided in two for a scrimmage. Darrell O'Reilly and Shel Nordstrom are the respective power forward and centre for the opposing team, and Leonard drives fearlessly through the lane and puts lay-up after lay-up over their outstretched hands.

The coach pats Leonard on the back after practice, but down in the locker room Darrell calls him a fucking fag who sucks dick for a living. The rest of the team breaks off their respective conversations and watches the two of them circle, but Leonard decides to just give Darrell the finger and dresses quickly so that nothing can transpire.

That night, Leonard prays to God to apologize for whatever sins are causing such disfavour. He knows the Lord is angry with him because he is getting Darrell to call Leonard a homosexual, even though he isn't because that would be against church doctrine. It occurs to Leonard that the Lord is simply testing his faith, like when he told Abraham to sacrifice his son Isaac and Abraham was ready to do it but then God was just kidding.

To prove that he is truly worthy of God's good will, Leonard decides that he will only walk on the white tiles of the school floor the next day.

The following morning, he gets off the bus and opens the school's front door. He realizes that he will have to go around back because there is a large section of red twenty steps deep in the entranceway. He excuses himself from a group of friends, saying he forgot something on the bus, and exits around the rear, where the chequered black and white tiles start immediately. He is forced to walk an irregular, focussed path to his homeroom, but arrives undaunted and saunters in carelessly because all of the classroom floors are painted white.

It isn't until the end of second period that he realizes in horror that the surface of every boys' bathroom is green. So he locks his legs together through Science class, cursing himself for stopping at the water fountain after Math, and realizing it takes a great deal of forethought to be a soldier for the Lord.

At lunch, he peels out the back entrance and runs all the way to Albert's Deli three blocks away, where he orders a ham and cheese sandwich in exchange for the use of their facilities. On the way back to school, Leslie Ann Hughes spots him and tells everyone that he is a loner because he was walking by himself.

"Why—did you break up with *Seleena*?" John jeers.

Everyone laughs and Leonard makes a mental note to continue pretending to be John's friend, and then invite him over for a sleepover and suffocate his fucking face with a pillow.

For the rest of the day the class makes jokes about how Leonard is an outcast with no life, and in Social Studies Chris Eagles compares him to post-World War Two Germany because no one wants to be his friend. Leonard looks out the window toward the schoolyard and tries to convince himself that everything is okay because Christian martyrs have always been mistreated. They've been stoned to death and fed to lions and burned at the stake and cooked in boiling oil and crucified upside down and beheaded, so he should never complain about being taunted for eating a deli sandwich alone at a window.

The rest of the day passes without incident, until Leonard retrieves his materials from his locker, standing with feet shoulder-width apart, each to its own white square, and two grade nine boys race down the hall and bowl into his shoulders. He wavers a moment before dropping back, considering how merciless the Lord can be, how he handed Job over to Satan just to prove a point, how his cattle were killed and his children were crushed and his wife gave up on him after he developed leprosy, and then Leonard looks down and the tip of his shoe is straddling the line between black and white.

LEONARD MUST NOT GO TO THE SCHOOL DANCE. He has failed the Lord and so he will no longer get to dance with Angela Watson, and the best that could happen would be to avoid being annihilated by God's wrath during

"Stairway to Heaven." The worst that could happen would be to have to slow dance with Janeen Winterston or Sarah Davenport while everyone watches and he loses the school's respect and everyone forgets he's the new star of the basketball team.

However, his father's excitement is its own beast.

"This is going to be the best day of your adolescence," he says, brandishing a twenty-dollar bill. "Here. I want you to spend all of it. I know it's not like nowadays you date or anything—but if you want to get a certain special someone a rose or something. Whatever's allowable according to the rules of cool."

"I don't feel good," says Leonard.

Leonard's father tells him it's nerves and that he should forget about it. He asks Leonard if he wants to get pumped up by listening to him recount the story of how he met their mother.

"At the zoo," says Leonard.

"And what happened?"

"She was there with another man and you told him the elephants were on the loose and he ran away."

"I love it!"

Steve points out that that story isn't even true, but their father says he's too young to be such a curmudgeon and shouldn't ruin Leonard's excitement.

"His first dance *ever*!"

"Will there be drugs?" asks Nick.

Their father looks down. "Who asks that when they're in grade five? No. There won't be drugs. They're illegal and make you go blind."

"Coffee's a drug," Steve points out.

"Coffee's a *legal* drug."

"John Erdos said that a mathematician was a device for turning coffee into theorems."

"See, there you go."

"But he took Ritalin every day."

"Well, he shouldn't have done that."

"But he proved the prime number theorem."

"And now he's probably dead."

"He died when he was eighty-three."

"Let's talk about something else."

"I want to take drugs, too!" says Nick.

"Okay," says their father. "Which drugs would you like to take?"

"The ones that make you go real fast so that you could win the one hundred metres at the Olympics."

"Ah," says their father. "But then you would be disqualified for doping."

"But you *could* take amphetamines and come up with mathematical theorems," says Steve. "And you wouldn't be disqualified for anything."

"Who cares!" says Nick. "Math sucks!"

"No," admonishes their father. "*Mathematicians* who do *drugs* suck. They set a very bad example for their students."

Leonard tells the family of a speech an ex-convict gave to his Health class earlier in the year. The man used to go to people's houses and take a crowbar to their kneecaps because he was a debt collector for a bicycle gang, so the motto was don't be a criminal.

"He said acid was the best drug in the world," says Leonard. "But we shouldn't do it or we'd start seeing groundhogs in our bathtubs."

"*Exactly*," says their father. "Now, you need to look good for the dance. Time to give you a shave."

"I have no facial hair," Leonard responds gloomily.

"I see a few whiskers. Let's lather you up."

Nick insists that he get to shave as well, and the three of them go into the bathroom together. Leonard examines the pinch in his father's plump cheeks, the merry bulbous nose protruding from the shaving cream. He realizes that he might have to go to the dance after all because he has promised the Lord that he would honour his father forever.

Nick applies a second coating of cream to his skin and says he's going to keep shaving until the end of the regular season, at which point he'll grow a playoff beard with the rest of the Calgary Flames.

"Good idea," says their father. "I'll do it too."

"Won't you get fired?"

"I guess. But Leonard's going to make the NBA."

"And I'm going to make the NHL," says Nick.

"And Steve is going to invent the next floppy disk," says their father. "So I have nothing to worry about."

But as his father drives him to the dance, Leonard thinks that his father has a lot to worry about. God is probably going to have Leonard stabbed at a urinal tonight, which will probably lead to his whole family suffering from depression. Nick and Steve will doubtless give up on their dreams and their mother will work even longer to avoid the stress. Then his parents will get divorced and his brothers will become drug addicts, so his father should stop acting so proud of him.

On the pretence of buying chewing gum, Leonard asks to be let off at the store nearest his school so that none of the kids get a good look at his father's fat. After Leonard gets out of the car he looks up at the thin sheet of his father's smile and wonders if he is dishonouring him with his shame, and if so that will be one more reason he will be on the Lord's hit list.

"Knock 'em dead!" his father calls out the window, and Leonard is left alone.

Inside, all the boys have come wearing their best button-up t-shirts. The girls are adorned in dresses and are dancing to "Thunderstruck" by AC/DC, which everyone agrees is awesome.

Leonard rationalizes that it will be harder for the Lord to strike him down if he is with a valorous person, so he seeks out Ron, who is at the very least studious because his parents are already putting pressure on him to graduate from dental school at McGill. But Ron is hanging out with a few others from his computer class, who also have moustaches, and Leonard thinks it is better to face God's wrath alone than to be seen in such company.

"Seleena is looking for you," Ron says.

Leonard does not want to see Seleena because she will want to dance with him during the slow songs and everyone will think they're dating, but she spots him immediately.

"I have to talk to you," she says.

"What is it?"

"I have to talk to you."

She drags him outside by the hand, which Leonard tries his best to avoid because it looks like they are leaving to go make out by the back steps near the smoke pit.

They get to the cafeteria and Seleena wheels around to tell him that Samantha has the hugest crush on him.

"*What?*"

She says that Samantha heard how good Leonard is at basketball and she thinks he's cute, especially when he wears his Hypercolor t-shirt. Leonard doesn't know what to do, although he is now incensed that he had decided against his Hypercolor in favour of the more traditional Ocean Pacific.

"*Well?*" asks Seleena.

Samantha is a new transfer from Cave Springs who takes Leonard's bus and is forced to sit up near the front even though she's in grade eight because all the seats have already been assigned. Every day she gets off at 7-Eleven and smokes while leaning against a pole with her head tilted to the side so that everyone can see all three of the piercings in her right ear.

The first day she had taken their bus, Ron had pointed at the back of her head for two minutes.

"Holy crap," he whispered, which were Leonard's feelings precisely. Leonard had thought about murdering Ron so that the seat beside him would be free, and if that was too evil, then maybe just breaking his finger so that he'd have to take a week off school.

"*Well?*"

Leonard says that of course he likes Samantha, and tells Seleena to march back onto the dance floor and tell her so. Seleena nods and as she leaves Leonard experiences a great swell of freedom in knowing that it no longer matters if people see the two of them together because soon he'll be dating one of the hottest chicks in the school, who is also a year older than him.

While Leonard waits for his big news he goes back into the gym to hang around near Mark. Mark's a great dancer and everyone is jealous of how good he is at doing the Worm, but Leonard could now care less if Mark could do the Moonwalk because it's not like he's the one dating Samantha from grade eight.

"Just wait till Kriss Kross comes on," Mark tells someone. Then he bobs his head like a duck and John tells him he's awesome.

Seleena returns again to give Leonard his coordinates.

"Samantha will be waiting under that basketball hoop," she says, pointing upward to their left.

Leonard thinks that if God really wanted to harm him he would destroy him right now with a heart attack. He watches the hoop thinking about how this is like a litmus test of God's approval because if he is really going to get to date Samantha, *Samantha* from grade *eight*, then the Lord must favour him regardless of his sins and approve of all of his honourable attempts in the past few weeks.

But then Leonard's heart sinks as he recalls the earlier promise he made to God—that if he were blessed with a girlfriend he would allow two weeks to pass before he tried to kiss her.

At first, Leonard tries to escape on a technicality. He argues that this was a promise made regarding Angela Watson, not Samantha. But he knows that the principles remain the same and that God is very much interested in principles, and plus, Samantha is even hotter than Angela Watson, so this is probably another test from the Lord to measure his piety.

It is a considerable trial. When at last "More than Words" plays out of the speakers Leonard walks towards the basketball hoop, feeling his heart in his knees. Samantha sidles up to him and he is suddenly closer to a girl than he ever has been before. He can feel the bulbs of her breasts pull back and push out against his ribcage as her hot breath floats in and out over his shoulder. He wants to bottle it and save it for later.

"Thank you," says Samantha, after the slow dance has ended.

"Yeah," says Leonard. "Do you want to go out with me?"

SEVEN DAYS LATER LEONARD AND SAMANTHA have their one-week anniversary. Leonard buys her a twenty-dollar gold brooch at Eaton's, plus a card he signs with Xs and Os after his name. She gets him the latest addition of *SLAM* magazine, featuring Joe Dumars. They trade presents in the alley behind 7-Eleven, and afterwards they hug.

Leonard goes home feeling warm inside, but later that night he gets a call from Seleena, who just talked to Samantha and she wanted to let him know that she is mad at him because she is used to dating boys her own age who aren't frigid.

"I'm not frigid!" Leonard says.

"Then how come you haven't kissed?"

Leonard has wanted to kiss Samantha, but he knows if he breaks his promise to God then the Lord will stop concentrating on the outcome of the Meech Lake Accord long enough to decimate his entire family. He has thought about telling Samantha he has a rare tongue disease that will suddenly evaporate in just one more week, but the next day Seleena passes him a note on the bus that says, *Sorry, Samantha dumped you. Crappy deal. Love, Seleena.*

When they get off the bus Samantha doesn't stop to smoke at 7-Eleven and heads home straight away. Leonard charges after her down an alley, throwing rocks at back fences behind her until she finally turns around to tell him he's immature.

"And you're a slut!" he responds.

The next day Samantha tells her good friend Josh Hamilton what Leonard had said and during lunch he slams Leonard's locker door in front of his face and challenges him to a fight off school grounds.

"Fuck off, I have basketball practice," Leonard says.

"You're fucking dead," Josh tells him.

Josh Hamilton is a grade nine rugby player with long

black hair like Kurt Russell's in *Tango & Cash*, so Leonard's first instinct is to feign a heart attack and explain to his teachers that it's a hereditary problem. But he knows this is not a viable long-term solution because the last grade seven to be challenged to a fight by an older student was Sean Alde, who phoned his mom and had her pick him up in person outside the door of his last class. To this day everyone laughs at him, so that he will never get a girlfriend until he moves to a university in another province, but even then he will have no experience with girls and say all the wrong things and probably commit suicide by jumping off the top of the office building where he works.

Leonard ducks out of the cafeteria midway through lunch and climbs four flights of stairs to the washroom near his art class, which nobody ever uses. There he prays for God to save him, until it comes to him that it is very common for the Lord to truly humble his servants before they can accept the righteous path. And knowing this, a strange peace comes over him, as he realizes that all that can be taken from him (his hockey card collection, his ability to play basketball, his well-shaped nose) is really nothing compared to all that is offered with eternity in God's kingdom in heaven.

So it is a remarkably tranquil Leonard who emerges from the upstairs washroom. And even that afternoon, when everyone looks his way in the hall and Samantha blows him a sardonic kiss and Darrell O'Reilly and Chris Eagles start a chant about how he will be bludgeoned to death, Leonard retains this peaceable demeanour. He does not flinch as the bell rings, and he smiles serenely at the older students charged with picking him up from his last class and escorting him three blocks off school property to the alley behind the liquor store.

By the time he arrives there is already a throng of students awaiting the inevitable. Leonard repeats the Lord's Prayer to himself and stands stoically as Josh Hamilton moves forward to distinguish himself from the others. He grabs Leonard by the collar and brings him forward, and Leonard's body is so relaxed that the movement is fluid and almost non-violent. Then there is a clap as Leonard's eye falls under Josh's fist, and next there are stars over shards of beer bottles and stone, and Leonard hits the ground so hard it is as if he is digging a hole for his knees to be buried in.

From the ground, looking up, Leonard considers his attacker and tries to remember the Lord. He looks out at the laughing masses and tries to recall how St. Sebastian was pierced by arrows for the sake of his faith, or how Peter pleaded to be crucified upside down so as not to be equated with Jesus, which was way worse because then all the blood ran to his head. But there were also the saints who survived, like John, who made it through being cooked in boiling oil, or those who were called forth to kick ass, like Joan of Arc pulling arrows out of her shoulder and running British people through with her sword.

And now Leonard is rising, seeming to himself very large, as though everything might fall away beneath him. He moves towards Josh Hamilton in a rage he considers a blessing, and when he starts in with his fists he finds it impossible to stop, so that only after the crowd is on him ten to an arm does he halt, and Josh Hamilton is in a very bad way. Leonard spots his opponent's face as he's led away, crowned the colour of royalty around the eyes, and suddenly doubts that this is what the Lord had in mind.

LEONARD'S MOTHER CONTINUES TO WORK long hours. Since he was not strong enough to accept his punishment at the hands of Josh Hamilton, Leonard imagines the Lord will become graver and make her the object of his wrath instead. So Leonard sits up every night, picturing his mother emerging from her downtown office building at three in the morning. She walks to her car swinging her keys around the swirl of her index finger before a wretched man from an alley swipes them and forces her to her vehicle. He unlocks it and throws her down in the back seat and the soil of his body dims the pale of her flesh as he pulls her panties down to her ankles and fucks her until it's like she's been broken in half.

Leonard battles every such thought with the Lord's Prayer, which their minister says is the most comprehensive of prayers and the only prayer Christ himself actually taught us. He enunciates all the words perfectly and focusses intently on their meaning so that the Lord might understand the depth of his devotion and spare his mother the fate of his sins. And even though this works at first, Leonard realizes that God has a great memory. He is all powerful and can do anything, like make a boulder so large that even he couldn't lift it, or have a piano fall randomly from the sky to squash an evil sinner, or have Leonard's mother raped if he made another mistake in his life—so Leonard must continue his prayers with devotion and consistency.

Leonard's mother works on Eighth Avenue and Sixth Street in a nice office building, but Leonard wants to know if she has an underground parking lot where she can store her Volkswagen so that she doesn't have to walk downtown at night and get carjacked. He also wants to know if there is a night code for her building or if any hobo off the street can simply walk into the lobby and wait for her to come down the elevator to threaten her with a knife.

One day Leonard looks up the exact address of Foster Parents Plan in the telephone book. After basketball practice he braves the cold and takes the LRT to his mother's building to see her surroundings first hand. He arrives, relieved to see that she is at the heart of the city centre, with the safe pedestrian walkway of Stephen Avenue one block behind her. She has taken herself out of harm's way and this makes it more likely that God will be forgiving because the Lord helps those who help themselves. Yet, in order to further protect her, Leonard places a small wooden cross in a box under a dumpster behind the alley of her building.

Every week Leonard makes his way out to this cross by his mother's office. He recites the Lord's Prayer five times in front of it, and each week his mother is spared.

Leonard comes every Monday because it is the one day he doesn't have basketball, though he tells his father that the coach has ordered extra practices to work on their motion offence.

One Monday, Leonard misses the bus that takes him from school to the LRT station, and so almost misses the 3:45 train that he has caught each week. He realizes that if he does not make this train the Lord will assume that he is very inept with sacrifices and obviously unconcerned about his mother's welfare and will have her raped as a lesson. So he jumps from the bus and shoots through the station, almost knocking over an old woman with a parcel under her arms (he feels bad for her, but at least she will not be raped), and plunges through the closing doors just as the train takes off downtown.

"Tickets, please!"

There is a policeman on the train collecting fares, which Leonard, in his haste, has forgotten to buy. The officer descends on Leonard and fines him one hundred and thirty-five dollars, due at the end of next month.

"I don't have one hundred and thirty-five dollars," says Leonard.

"Then you should have bought a ticket," says the officer.

Leonard thinks the officer should shut the fuck up and die, but he keeps quiet because he knows the Lord now wants him to receive his punishments calmly.

For the length of the trip downtown, Leonard wonders how he will come up with one hundred and thirty-five dollars if he's supposed to honour his father and is not even allowed to steal from him. But on the back of the ticket Leonard reads that community service hours are accepted in lieu of payment, and realizes that this must be the Lord's hidden message in the ordeal.

Next week, Leonard gets a volunteer position with the Red Cross, which is two blocks from his mother's office. His job is to telephone people who have given blood in the past and remind them to donate again or else people will die and it will be on their conscience. He comes in every Monday after praying at his mother's building and quite enjoys his job because he no longer has to lie to his father about having an extra basketball practice. Instead, he can continue to honour him by explaining that he has decided to start volunteering at the Red Cross because it is an admirable organization whose mission is to improve the lives of vulnerable people by mobilizing the power of humanity.

"I'm proud of you," their father tells Leonard. "You guys hear this? About Leonard volunteering? That's an example you should follow."

"I'm too busy," says Steve.

"What's in it for me?" asks Nick.

"What's in it for you is helping others less fortunate," says their father. "How about that?"

"That sounds boring," says Nick.

"It's actually very rewarding," says Leonard, proudly, but not too proudly, because pride is sinful.

LEONARD'S CLASS CONTINUES TO MAKE FUN of him for being frigid. One day, after Darrell O'Reilly lets a pencil fall against his desk and calls it Leonard's penis, Leonard gets so upset he yells at Janeen Winterston to stop laughing because she's so ugly she better get rich to pay male hookers to fuck her because no one would ever do it for free. And then everybody stops laughing because Janeen has a problem with acne and no one has dared to make fun of her since her mother phoned in to complain about the merciless treatment Janeen was receiving. Her mother told the teacher about all the drugs Janeen was taking to clear her face and all their bad side effects, like how they burn Janeen's cheeks and make her depressed and might even increase her chances of having a stroke. So one day the teacher excused Janeen and kept everyone in after class and told them they should all be ashamed of themselves, and afterwards even Darrell shuffled his feet down the hall.

"You're a little shit, McKinley," Brent says, but then the teacher interrupts them asking for an example of alliteration.

"Catherine cried quietly," Janeen says.

Leonard looks over and sees her mouth wide open like a cockleshell, her cheeks flushed like she'd been caught in the wind.

"Excellent," says their teacher.

When Leonard goes home he remembers the story Mark and John had told him about the fat girl from Kenmore who was teased so much she finally broke down and threw herself in front of a passing car because someone said her dog looked like a rat. Leonard imagines Janeen Winterston doing the same sort of thing, and there being an article in the paper the next day in which everyone testifies to the fact that Leonard told her she would have to depend on male prostitutes for the rest of her life, so he promises on the spot that from that moment on he will be completely and utterly good.

So the next morning when Nick starts to spy on him from behind a fortress of cereal boxes, Leonard simply smiles. At lunch, he buys a chocolate bar from the cafeteria and splits it four ways, and during French class he volunteers to pair up with Kyle McDonald, even though Leonard ends up completing the exercise himself because Kyle is stupid and doesn't know any of the answers.

On the way home that day, Julie Hinton and Jennifer O'Shea scream shrilly from the back of the bus because there are two hot boys following them in their Toyota. Julie stands and unbuckles her belt so that she can moon them, and when she does Ron cranes his neck as far it can go to the right-hand side.

"I saw a piece of her ass," he tells Leonard.

Leonard doesn't look because God would be disappointed in him, even though Julie has a great ass. It is best for Leonard to defend Christian principles, and so later when John starts talking about fucking his girlfriend, Leonard musters his courage and tells him he shouldn't talk like that because pre-marital sex is immoral.

John kills himself laughing. "*Frigid*!"

"You're not Christian, what do you know?" says Leonard.

But John says that's not true because you can just disagree with some parts of the Bible and believe in others, and he disagrees with the part about pre-marital sex because what's the difference anyways. Leonard says the difference is the sacred union between a man and a woman sanctified by God, and that you can't just take out the parts of the Bible that you like because that's not the way it works.

"Of course it is," John says. "Like how it says that God made the earth in seven days and science says that it's impossible, so some of it's just a story."

"You don't know anything about science."

"*Whatever.* What about David and Goliath—it's not true that Goliath was ten feet, it's just to show the underdog can win."

"Goliath could have been ten feet because God can do anything," Leonard says.

John says that if God can do anything how come he doesn't stop all the wars in the world and how come everyone in Africa is starving.

"I don't know," says Leonard. "Maybe you can ask him before he sends you to burn in hell."

"At least I have a girlfriend," John says.

When he gets home, Leonard borrows Steve's paperback edition of the *Guinness Book of World Records* and finds out that the tallest man in recorded history was Robert Wadlow at eight foot eleven, who died in

1940. The next day he shows it to John as proof that Goliath could have been as tall as the Bible says.

"Then how come Goliath's not in there?" asks John.

Leonard says that in biblical times they didn't have measuring tape, so the *Guinness Book of World Records* probably wouldn't accept Goliath's submission on technical grounds.

"But it shows that it's still possible for people to be that tall."

John calls him immature and says that even if Goliath was that tall he would have been super skinny and had a heart condition and so would have been easy to beat up anyways.

"My grandfather has a heart condition," says Ron. "And anyone could beat him up."

"*See*?" says John, and starts talking about fucking his girlfriend again.

Leonard thinks to tell them that they don't know anything about heart conditions because his father suffers from one and has almost died, and then John would feel sorry for him and never call him frigid again. But Leonard abstains and continues on the virtuous path because he knows it keeps his mother safer than ever. The Lord will not have her raped when she has a volunteering son who defends the Lord's doctrines in public, especially while there are other mothers with useless bums for sons like Darrell O'Reilly, Shel Nordstrom, Brent Campbell and Chris Eagles.

So even after his traffic fine has been paid in full, Leonard continues to man the telephones at the Red

Cross. He comes to school every morning with an increasing sense of confidence that God is about to destroy all his enemies, and sure enough, only two weeks before the start of Cypress Groves' playoff run, Darrell O'Reilly charges the lane in basketball practice and breaks his ankle.

Leonard's father is dismayed.

"He was your best rebounder!" he says, after Leonard gleefully announces the news. "What are you guys going to do in the paint?"

"I'll take care of it," says Leonard.

"But you're the point guard. You can't do everything! You're already leading the team in points, assists, steals—everything else! You need some help out there!"

"This is the inherent difficulty of team competition," says Steve thoughtfully. "That's why I steer clear of it."

"You don't play because you suck," says Nick.

"*Hey*!" says their father. "Steve doesn't suck. He was awesome at his last science fair. First place! Next up, provincial exams!"

His father gives Steve a high five, forcing Nick to point out that he is already playing in a hockey age group two brackets above his own.

"Don't I know it," says their father, "but let's not compete here. You're all awesome!"

Their mother had said the same thing a few weeks earlier after Steve had shown everyone his newest painting, which he said was representative of his heart.

"This is very unique, Steven," said their father. "I like the shards of glass."

Their mother said that Steve had the heart of a poet, and that there would never be a reason to worry about him because he would always find inspiration from any situation he was faced with in life.

Nick pointed out that the same was true of him because he had just written a story for his grade five class called "Who Killed Michael Jordan?" that received an A plus.

"A real page turner," said their father.

"Do you remember the part where Michael Jordan is in a coma but at the end breaks out of in the fourth quarter of the finals so that he can shoot the winning basket against the Lakers? And then the Lakers get deported to Spain and have to play in the European league, which sucks."

"That's right!"

"I thought the story was called, 'Who *Killed* Michael Jordan?'" asked Steve.

"It is," said Nick.

"Then how could he still be alive at the end to shoot the winning basket?"

"No, they just think he's dead because someone broke into his house and shot him, and then he went into a coma."

"Then he's not *dead*," said Steve. "You should have called it 'Who Put Michael Jordan in a Coma?'"

"That's stupid!"

"Well, it's the difference between existence and non-existence."

"No, it's not!"

Their father told them to knock it off, but Nick wanted to know if he had the heart of a poet as well.

"No," said Steve. "Only *I* write poetry."

"You all have the heart of a poet," said their mother. "Now let's eat."

Leonard sat and thought about the fact that now that he was volunteering, it would be okay to start dating again. Even though there was still a rumour going around that he was frigid, the fact that he gave Josh Hamilton a black eye in the alley and scored forty points against St. Stephen's had given Leonard numerous opportunities to date girls. Josephine Diamond, Hilary Webster and Meghan Black all went on record as saying they liked him. But to ensure that his mother stayed healthy, Leonard passed on every opportunity.

Now, however, Leonard could take his new girlfriend to the Red Cross. He could show her where everyone gives blood and where some people pass out because their blood pressure drops. Then she could watch him play basketball and he could look to her for inspiration if he ever needed to score an extra basket in the dying seconds of the game.

In order to display his fairness to the Lord, Leonard picks the girl who liked him from the start, and he and Meghan go out to a movie on a Saturday night. They see *A League of their Own* starring Tom Hanks and Madonna, about two sisters on a women's baseball team during World War Two. At the end of the movie the sisters are on opposing teams and have a run-in at the plate, and Leonard gets angry because the snotty sister bowls over the good sister so that the wrong team ends up winning.

"That's life," shrugs Meghan.

Leonard thinks that Meghan obviously doesn't believe in God because if she did she would realize that the Lord would either give the good sister glory by making the snotty sister trip over her own feet in front of the entire stadium, or at worst have the good sister tortured and executed for her Christianity but still go down in history as a saint.

But Leonard does not correct Meghan in this matter because she has started to hold his hand as they pass through the parking lot towards the LRT station. The odd car rushes past, heading into the city in the quiet night, and the two of them fall into silence knowing this is the moment they are to turn to each other. And Leonard knows that this is not okay with God, especially if Meghan's not Christian, he knows the Lord doesn't want him making out with anyone, period, especially not with heathens—but now the station is upon them and there is no reason to keep moving so that they are leaning in. And before the Lord's Prayer is on Leonard's tongue there is the strong scent of strawberries and kiwi and everything warm and wet instead.

LEONARD ARRIVES HOME TO AN EMPTY HOUSE. The first thing he notes is that Captain does not dash to the door to greet him, and so he figures that everyone must be at

Uncle Bob's. Uncle Bob is lonely and lives by himself, so he likes it when the whole family comes over so that he can pat Captain and play chess with Steve and feed sugar to Nick.

Leonard lies back on the couch and tries to apologize to God for being sexual, but in reality he feels good because now everyone at school will stop calling him frigid and comparing his dick to a wilted flower.

He is lying on the couch watching *Quantum Leap* when the family comes home an hour later and tries to calm him at once.

"Don't worry, honey," says their mother. "Everything's *fine*."

"He's okay," affirms their father.

"Did you get my note?" cuts in Nick, carrying Captain in his arms.

"What note?"

"I left it in your bedroom."

"Oh, Nick," cries their mother. "Why didn't you leave it in the kitchen?"

"There were some complications with Captain," says their father.

"The vet showed me the anaesthesia machine," says Steve.

Leonard bolts upright. "What complications?"

"You see, here he is, he's *fine*," says their mother.

Nick leans over to show him. Captain stares out vacantly from beyond the tuft of his matted nose. He pants in greeting, looking the same as always.

"What?" asks Leonard.

Their father explains that he had suffered an epileptic fit.

"His eyes rolled back in his head!" shouts Nick.

"*Nick!*" says their mother.

"Common during a generalized seizure," says Steve.

"The dog had an epileptic fit?!" yells Leonard.

"*Generalized seizure,*" repeats Steve. "It's good because he loses consciousness—"

"He *lost consciousness*!?"

"And respiration stops."

"Steve!" says their mother.

"*He wasn't breathing?*"

"He's fine," says their mother.

"Look—he's alive!" says their father.

"For about thirty seconds," says Steve, answering Leonard's question. "Then the clonic phase begins."

"*Ahh…*"

"Oh sweetheart, don't worry," says their mother.

"It's very common in dogs," says their father.

"He peed all over the rug!" says Nick excitedly.

"Nick, it *doesn't matter,*" says their mother. "He's fine. The doctor says that he will probably live the same life as before."

"*Probably?*" exclaims Leonard.

"Certainly!" says their father.

"Depending on the frequency of the seizures," says Steve.

"One thing at a time…" says their mother.

"It's going to happen *again?*" asks Leonard.

"Yes," says Steve.

"No," say his parents.

"Maybe?" asks Nick.

"*What*?"

Their mother sighs. "Probably."

Leonard's shoulders tumble.

"But honey, it doesn't mean anything. It's actually not that bad."

"His eyes rolled back in his head!" says Leonard, disbelieving.

"And his legs went straight like he was dead," adds Nick, sticking his arms out and nearly dropping the dog.

"Nick!" says their father.

"But there are *signs*," says their mother. "Now we know when it's coming. So we can take him in before it happens again and he'll be fine. Just like he was this time. And that's even *if* it happens again."

"It will!" says Nick, now certain. "But who cares, Captain's amazing! He could probably survive double!"

"You bet!" says their father.

"Let's up the voltage!" says Nick.

The family sits to discuss the matter quickly before bed time, but tempers are short. When Steve lists off the warning signs—how Captain will pace, salivate, or whine before his next seizure, Nick becomes frustrated because he doesn't understand.

"He does those things anyways!"

"Yes, but…"

"What's the difference between normal whining and seizure whining?"

"Oh, of course there'll be a difference!" snaps their mother.

"Well I want to know what!" says Nick.

"Well, *listen*!"

"How about we talk about this in the morning?" says their father.

"But what if Captain dies in the night?" asks Leonard.

"Oh, he's not going to die in the night!" exclaims their mother.

"How do you know?"

"Because seizures come far apart!"

"But what if they don't?"

"Well, what if we all get steamrolled by a train!" their mother cries.

Their father claps his hands together and officially closes the family meeting until the morning—"barring accidental deaths." Leonard pities the lot of them because they don't understand how close they all actually are to being steamrolled, because they have a sinner for a sibling who has kissed a heathen, and so immediately God has struck Captain down with an epileptic fit. And perhaps this is only the beginning.

Leonard mounts the stairs thinking about poor Captain with his legs fired out rigid across the carpet. How he was knocked unconscious and almost extinguished from the earth, and how for the rest of his life he will suffer from such violent attacks—all because Leonard wanted to become worldly. And it seems unfair that the Lord would take his displeasure out on the most harmless of all creatures and for a moment Leonard curses God and thinks he hates him.

But then he thinks he was just kidding and he doesn't hate God at all, he loves God: *God is the best, God is great*. But a thought is there within him again: *I love Satan*, and Leonard thinks immediately, *that's not true*, he hates Satan.

I love Satan—NOT, he repeats, adding the qualifier; *I love Satan—NOT*. But then he thinks, *I hate God*, and the whole thing repeats once more.

I rail against Satan according to all that is within me, Leonard thinks, slamming the door to his room. He thinks that if he were in the desert with the sand swept before him on all sides and he had yet to eat for forty days and the devil offered him the stone to make bread he would cast it aside. And if Satan took him to the pinnacle overlooking the roofs of the Holy City and told him to jump in expectation that the Lord would break his fall, he would not commit hubris and put his God to the test. And if Satan took him to the mountaintop and offered him all the kingdoms of the world for his adulation he would order him away for it is said to worship the Lord your God and serve him only.

But Leonard has not served the Lord and so the angels will not attend to him. He has allowed the blasphemy inside and so now it is to be wrung out by the Lord as in the exorcising of a demon, and it will be long and hard, and his body and mind will fail him as the devil takes him over and acts from within.

He rips a poster from his wall thinking again that he

loves Satan, and no, again, that he does *not*, and wonders if he has just made himself a sinner. He thinks about the people who wrote the Bible, if they wrote that *thou shall not commit adultery* then they must have thought about committing adultery, or at least about someone else committing adultery. But they didn't think, *I love adultery*, Leonard thinks—but then he worries that he has just thought that he loves adultery, even though he doesn't and if his Dad ever had sex with another woman he would never speak to him again and break his legs.

I love adultery—Not, Leonard thinks, and then back and forth so hard he could crush a coin in his teeth. For the rest of the night he wonders about his level of damnation because he knows that in Hebrews it says that God judges the thoughts and attitudes of the heart, but it does not specify how long it takes for a thought to get into our heart, or how long a thought takes to become an attitude, or even what the difference between the two is. I love Satan—Not, he thinks, wondering what that means, if it was possible to love Satan within a second, even if he didn't, did not, not, *not...*

On Leonard's pillow there is a note from Nick, offhandedly remarking that the dog just croaked.

Part Three

THE ENTIRE CAMP IS LISTENING TO Adam Wilson sing "Go Tell It on the Mountain," but Leonard swears he isn't interested and so decides to hum something else under his breath. The first thing to come to mind is "Freshman" by Vervepipe, which they played at his high school graduation to symbolize a rite of passage, even though it's actually about a guy asking his girlfriend to get an abortion so they don't have to get married. Leonard refuses to bow to peer pressure as all the other summer camp counsellors join Adam on the last chorus, and continues humming to himself even through the final crescendo and the campers' applause.

Then the campfire breaks and Adam roars past him carrying two grade five campers, on one each arm, passing close to Leonard's shoulder so that he has to shift just in time to avoid Adam's contact.

Leonard starts off to his own cabin. Nick is at his side, loudly fantasizing about how awesome it would be to shatter Adam's guitar by slamming it over his head until he was unconscious.

"I *hate* that song about the mountain!" he exclaims, arguing that the camp rule should be that you have to play something good like Pearl Jam or you get smashed into the ground.

"It's *fine*," says Leonard.

"I say we destroy him."

Leonard feels bad because Nick is just frustrated because he is supposed to be off training for his upcoming season with the Brandon Wheat Kings. He was taken thirtieth overall in the WHL entry draft, but at the end of the season he suffered a groin injury and has to spend the summer rehabilitating. As a result, he has been forced up to Saskatchewan with the rest of the family to spend the summer at their cottage in Waskesiu. Since there is no town except for Prince Albert within miles of their cottage, it is almost impossible to get a summer job, especially for a fifteen-year-old like Nick with no experience beyond the rink. Leonard pulled some strings at the Bible camp he had worked at the previous summer so that Nick could be hired on as an activities co-coordinator.

"But I hate preteens!" said Nick. "They're like eunuchs with hormones."

Regardless, Nick didn't have any other options. Now, he and Leonard part for their own cabins. Leonard gives his campers the five-minute warning before he shuts out all of the lights. The boys scramble away from their illegal card game and scurry into bed. With one minute still remaining, Leonard pulls the cord and the cabin descends into darkness.

Leonard mounts his bunk and leads his campers in the Lord's Prayer. Their voices drift drearily into the distance until they are incoherent utterances under the trees, and once they are complete Leonard does not continue alone.

>⊶⌁⊷<

IN THE MORNING, LEONARD'S PARENTS ARRIVE for chapel at the camp. Steve joins them after the service because he has not been a Christian for years. After his first semester of university he came home at Thanksgiving and told the family that he didn't believe in God because science had proved that the universe began fourteen billion years ago. While he rambled on about Hubble's Law and the cosmological principle and the infinite density of black holes, Leonard and Nick ducked behind their plates and waited for objects to start smashing, but their father only shovelled potatoes into his mouth.

"You're an adult now," said their mother. "Do as you please."

Afterwards Nick kicked a wall in frustration. "I thought they were going to slaughter him," he said, disappointed.

This summer, Leonard's parents are excited because Steve has come back from Texas to stay with them. He usually spends the entire year at the university, but this summer his girlfriend is working overseas, and the cottage is a quiet place for him to write his Master's thesis on Computer Human Interface.

"A genius!" their father says. "I don't even know what that means!"

Now, their mother asks them how camp is going.

"Shoot me," says Nick.

"Fine," says Leonard.

"That baptism sucked," says Nick. "The baby didn't even cry."

Their father assents. "Remarkably calm."

"I think they should make them more interesting," continues Nick. "Like they should put the baby in one of those dunking tanks and then the parents could throw apples at the target to see if the baby gets saved or not."

Nick doesn't care much about religion, but regards it as an effective time waster. Whenever he runs out of activities with his campers he asks, "Who's better: God or Jesus? *Discuss*," and encourages them to fight.

The family eats barbeque lunch with the rest of the parishioners and listens to Steve explain about Muslim pilgrimages to Zamzam, and how they believe that the wells there are blessed and cure illnesses.

"When, in fact, it's probably due to the fact that the water contains unusually high levels of calcium and fluoride," he says.

"Well, that's really something," says their father, studying his burger with delight.

"*Great*," says Nick, either in reference to the conversation or the fact that Adam Wilson is approaching their table.

"Uh-oh," says their father jovially, also spotting him. "My competition."

Adam laughs gregariously. "Don't tease me, Doug!"

Even though Adam is only eighteen, Leonard's father always kids their mother about her being infatuated with Adam because she once said he had hair like a little sunflower. Adam stands beside their table looking tall, strong and bronze, though Leonard cannot be sure because he does not look up. He watches his mother blossom before him.

"*Helllooo, Adam*," she says, with feigned excitement.

"*Oh*, I'm melting!" Adam exclaims.

Leonard watches Nick's fist ball beneath the table.

"Hey, guys!" Adam greets them.

Leonard and Nick nod wearily at the table; Steve rises to shake his hand.

"It's good to see you guys out today," he says.

"Are you kidding?" Leonard's father exclaims. "I can't keep her away from you!"

"Oh, that's enough!" says their mother.

"When I die," says their father, teasing Adam. "But only then. And that doesn't mean I want to go prematurely, all right? Don't start concocting any crazy schemes or anything. You've got maybe twenty years on me—you can wait me out! Then, she's all yours!"

"Shut up, Dad," Nick says.

"I'd like to be buried at sea," their father continues, philosophically.

"If you were Muslim," says Steve, still on the former thread, "the expenses would be tax deductible."

"Well, there you go!" says their father. "Perhaps

I'll switch. No, just kidding, Adam! All hail the Lord, right?"

Leonard was originally employed by Camp Duchesne last summer, after his father hired Adam to clean their eavestroughs while they were gone in the winter. His father had met Adam in the supermarket after Adam had recommended the cantaloupe because it was delicious. Leonard's father struck up a conversation and hired him on the spot, and Leonard had met him when he came around a few weeks later to look at the house. When Leonard learned that Adam worked at Camp Duchesne they bonded over religion and the power of the Holy Spirit. Adam told Leonard that God had saved him from Internet gambling and Leonard told Adam that God had kept his dog alive in spite of epilepsy, so the two of them were inseparable for the rest of the summer break. Adam got him a job at the camp for the final few weeks of last August and a full-time job starting this year.

Adam even did Leonard the favour of getting Nick hired, even though Adam and Nick hate one another. When they first met, Nick learned that Adam also had two brothers, so he asked him which he would rather kill.

"Neither," said Adam. "Murder's a sin."

"I'd kill Leonard," said Nick, "because Steve would cry too much and make me feel bad."

Then Nick had tried to get Adam to play a game he invented called suicidal croquet, which involves golfing with croquet mallets and hammering balls through clumps of trees as hard as you could.

"I don't know about that," said Adam.

"What do you like to do?"

"Dance," said Adam.

Nick killed himself laughing. "I would rather people threw bricks at my head than be caught clacking my heels with a cane!"

"I don't mean that kind—"

"Canes are only good for taking people out at the knees!"

Leonard's relationship with Adam has been rocky this season as well, since Leonard cannot look at him without thinking homosexual thoughts. Two days after he had arrived at camp, Leonard was standing out on the counsellors' porch with Adam beside him, talking about the contrast between the seasons in Saskatchewan and how lucky he was to be blessed with vacations in a province that fosters a full appreciation for the diversity of God's creation. Adam puzzled over how understanding the Lord was just like attempting to count all the stars in the sky, which was not a form of counting at all, but a challenge to strive for a sense of completion in the face of the impossible.

"The beautiful thing about it is that we'll never be short of work," he said.

Despite a recent surge of religious doubt, Leonard was struck by the profundity of this statement. Of how it is good to revel in the beauty of the sky and to seek to understand even a little of its intricacies, just as it was good to revel in the beauty of the Lord's complexity rather than turn oneself away from the task on the grounds that it could never be done. Swept up in the idea, he turned to Adam and accidentally caught him leaning back, basking in the heat of the sun, his arms golden over the length of his torso, the lines on his pelvis extending underneath his swimming trunks. And then Leonard thought that he was revelling in the body of a man and was therefore gay.

Back at the chapel, Adam leaves to go show Leonard's parents the new floating dock he's building for the campers.

"If he asked me to go, I'd smash a loose board over his head," says Nick.

"*So* friendly," says Steve.

Nick says that he and Adam should have a tug-of-war where the winner gets to dictate the country that the other would live in for the rest of their existence.

"Lithuania has the world's highest suicide rate," says Steve.

"I'll send him there," Nick says firmly.

"Isn't Melinda from Eastern Europe?" Steve asks Leonard.

"Yeah," says Leonard. "Her father lived under Communists. They weren't even allowed to listen to jazz."

"Wait. What about if I put him in Antarctica?"

"He would be lonely," says Steve.

"What's its population?" Nick asks.

"I would imagine it would depend on whether it's winter or summer."

"I thought it was always winter."

"That would be impossible."

"Well what's the maximum amount of people?"

Steve considers. "Couldn't be over five thousand."

Nick nods fiercely. "That's good. Cold and lonely."

"I don't know if he'll agree to the terms," says Steve.

"Because he's chicken," says Nick, grudgingly.

<hr />

AT NIGHT LEONARD LAYS AWAKE IN HIS BUNK, staring up at the long wood planks on the ceiling, imagining they are penises and trying to figure out if he wants to put them in his mouth. He constantly imagines Adam with his shirt off to see if this sexually excites him; he pictures sucking on his dick and getting fucked in the ass and turning him around to reciprocate.

The thoughts continue to terrify him until at last he tries to stop thinking about them. But in each spare moment he wants to discover the truth about himself, and so he imagines men fornicating together one last time, to see if he can't at last discover how he *actually* feels. And each time he has no idea, and each time he keeps imagining is sworn to be the last. It is the last time when he imagines gay sex while the counsellors play Frisbee, the last time when he thinks of sucking cocks during baptism, the last time as he listens to his brothers argue about where to exile Adam while Leonard considers kissing the soft back of his neck above the bubbles in a hot tub.

"Adam's such a dickweed," says Nick. "I hate how Dad offered him Mom's hand in marriage after he gets murdered."

"I don't think that's what he meant," says Steve.

"Like as if he could ever murder Dad. If he ever murdered Dad I would sneak into the same jail and bench press him."

"Right."

"Not that he ever could murder Dad, because if he tried, Dad would just have a heart attack before Adam could even get the satisfaction of stabbing him."

Leonard's father had another heart attack two years ago in his bedroom before he went to sleep. He complained to their mother of chest pains, and thinking it was just stiffness in his joints, started doing push-ups to loosen up. The ambulance was called a few minutes later, but he was back within a day.

Their mother, shaken, put a chain across the pantry. Their father pointed out he was no worse than the dog, and was even a tad triumphant when Captain eclipsed him with a third epileptic fit.

Nick said that their father should make sure to do push-ups during his next heart attack because it brought good luck and would set a unique world record. Plus, it was hardcore and it impressed Nick's personal trainer, who once worked out alongside Steven Seagal.

After their father's most recent heart attack, Leonard went into the basement and pierced through his thigh with a dart. He knew that his father's suffering was of his account, though the only noteworthy sin he could recall of late was that he coveted his friend Edward's girlfriend, Patrice. But Leonard's entire class coveted her, it was quite natural, she had an ass as round as an earlobe, and none of the other students had fathers dropping nearly dead from heart attacks. Moreover, his father had his first heart attack when Leonard was only six. While everyone is born sinful and the Lord works in mysterious ways, Leonard figures this probably had less to do with any offence he had committed at such a young age, and more to do with the fact that his father sometimes ate a half-dozen bratwurst sausages in a sitting.

Over the course of many months, Leonard began to second guess his religion, even though he didn't want to because if God did exist and Leonard wasn't a believer he would burn in hell for eternity, which was an incredibly long time. Sometimes, when Leonard was saying the Lord's Prayer and came to, *"thine is the kingdom, the power and the glory, forever and ever,"* he tried to imagine what infinity actually meant. Steve once told him that, mathematically speaking, given infinity, a monkey typing randomly at a computer would eventually write all of *Hamlet* by accident. (Nick said it didn't matter because even given infinity a monkey could never score a goal against him because he had an amazing glove hand.)

Leonard tries to imagine his skin on fire forever. He lies very still and focusses intently on how it would feel to burn for five seconds. Then he multiplies this by larger periods of time, like how long his forefathers had lived and all the years the dinosaurs had roamed the earth. Then he fast forwards to the future and imagines what might occur: superhumans and robot drones and another ice age, and throughout all of this he must burn. And even if he gets used to the pain he's sure the Lord will vary it so that he is always suffering in new and unique ways, until at last a monkey finishes *Hamlet*, and even then it would continue.

***

AT THE END OF THE SECOND WEEK OF CAMP Nick organizes a fire along the beach and invites everyone except Adam Wilson, who shows up nonetheless, guitar in hand. Undeterred, Nick tells everyone a ghost story about a man who gets trapped alone in the wilds of Antarctica, and because he is a wimp and can't hunt like a real man he is forced to eat his own flesh. He eats first from his buttocks, but second, because he lacks forethought, each of his own fingers. But then he is stuck with no way to cut off the rest of his flesh and so, like a dummy, he slowly starves to death in agonizing pain.

The campfire reacts with silence.

"There isn't even a ghost in that story," says Silvia, another counsellor.

So Nick invents a spontaneous ending where the man turns into a phantom and goes looking for his guitar but finds it smashed over his own dead corpse.

"The End," he finishes.

"But how did his guitar get to Antarctica?" Silvia demands.

"That's the mystery," says Nick.

Silvia says that it is a dumb story and asks Adam to play something on his guitar instead. Adam plays

"Round Here" by Counting Crows and at the end of the night he and Silvia are the last two by the fire.

Nick walks home in the dark with Leonard, complaining that he doesn't understand women. He says Steve is awesome because he's his brother, but he never would have thought him capable of dating someone like his girlfriend, Ilyana, who stops all the trucks in Calgary each time she comes home to visit the family with him.

"And your girlfriend is beautiful, too," says Nick, with disgust, "and all you play is *basketball*. I'm a goalie in the WHL! This is *Canada*. I should be like royalty!"

"Maybe your modesty turns them off," says Leonard.

"I *hate* Adam Wilson and his stupid guitar!" Nick cries to the trees.

Melinda Pajak, Leonard's girlfriend, is very beautiful. One counsellor told him she was hotter than God, plus she is hilarious because she was always telling awesome stories about shooting her Dad in the head playing paintball or how her brother sounded like a sheep when he stuck his hand in a socket and got electrocuted.

When they first met at the beginning of the summer, Melinda had gone down on Leonard out on the beach among the rocks. Leonard had held tight to their jagged edges and swayed with the waves, finally closing his eyes over the last porch light in bliss. But now he can't even kiss her because he thinks about being gay.

Leonard is confused because he doesn't know if he makes out with Melinda and then gets a boner if that will be due to his being excited by her or his recent homosexual thoughts, and then he won't know whether he is gay or straight. And if he's gay there's technically nothing wrong with that—there was a PRIDE society at his school that taught him to say that homosexuals are equal—but it's still not expedient. It will make it hard to be accepted by the church, plus it will be awkward on his basketball teams because they were very much heterosexual, and his life in general will need a huge overhaul because people would constantly be making jokes behind his back.

But if Leonard simply gives up and doesn't touch Melinda then this will only push him towards being gay. So he knows he must continue to be physical with her, and this is what he somehow plans to accomplish tomorrow after they finish mini-golfing with her family in Waskesiu. Leonard knows that it is simply a matter of determination. He has a three-stage plan to kiss Melinda with purity. First, he must focus solely on her and think normal heterosexual thoughts, like how her breasts are amazing. Then, he must hold her afterwards and think only of how romantic and normal it is. Third, if gay thoughts come to mind, he must shut his eyes and tap his head twice, remembering that he and Melinda are as one, and she will let him know himself and the world around him once again.

Leonard says goodnight to Nick and reunites with his campers, though he cannot join them in slumber because he thinks and thinks and *thinks.*

⟩⟨

MELINDA'S LITTLE BROTHER, NELSON, lines up his putt. Leonard examines his soft hands shifting on the grip of the shaft and looks away towards the course's club house. There is an old woman inside buying potato chips. He watches her instead.

"I think, perhaps, this will be a hole in one," Mr. Pajak tells his son.

"*Shhh*, he's trying to putt," says Mrs. Pajak.

"Oh yes, I see. Which is why I point out that it will soon be a hole in one."

"Well, let him do it, then. C'mon Nelson, there are others waiting their turn."

"Do not hit the windmill!" Mr. Pajak points out. "You must time your shot."

"Dad, he knows," says Melinda.

"*Oh*. While you are in front you can be confident, but not all of us are so fortunate."

"It's only the fourth hole."

"I am well aware. A good a time as any to break for the lead."

"Can he not putt, please?" says Mrs. Pajak.

Leonard looks back as Nelson follows through on his stroke. His ball is in line with the hole in the middle of the windmill, but one of the revolving arms descends in time to block its entrance. The ball ricochets back to the start line.

"Ah, but you have failed!" says Mr. Pajak.

"Melinda, you're next," states Mrs. Pajak.

"Sorry," says Nelson to the family.

"It is a perfectly straight shot," says Mr. Pajak, shaking his head. "I don't understand."

Melinda takes her turn in the tee box. Leonard eyes her long, toned legs as she putts through, winding himself up to think of her, *only her*…and then Mr. Pajak is putting next, measuring the break by bending at the knee, closing one eye, and gauging it with his putter.

"It's fine, Dad," says Melinda.

"Tut-tut," responds their father, thoughtfully rubbing the tip of his chin.

"*Dear*," says Mrs. Pajak.

"Well I can hardly waste the shot, can I?"

At long last, he gets into his stance and putts. His ball bounces back.

"Confound this windmill!" he cries.

"Next," says Mrs. Pajak.

"It's on some sort of irregular pattern," he insists.

"It's always the same," says Melinda.

"Listen," says their father, warning her with his finger. "I will have no bragging on the miniature golf course."

"I'm not bragging!"

"If not all of us are up to your speed then there is no need to be frustrated."

"I'm not frustrated!"

"You sound *quite* frustrated."

"Nelson, you again," says Mrs. Pajak.

Nelson eventually putts and breaks through to the other side. It takes Mr. Pajak another three attempts, during which he accuses the windmill of being manned via satellite. He ends the hole having shot six.

"Seven," argues Melinda.

"I'm sorry?"

"It was seven. Four to get through, as well as two missed putts on the other side. That's seven."

"You have no confidence in your father, is that it?"

"I'm just saying. You can't cheat."

"You are not better than me because you shot four," says Mr. Pajak.

"Three."

"What's that?"

"I shot three."

"And you claim you are not boastful."

Leonard walks at the rear of the group so as to avoid being targetted by one of Mr. Pajak's characteristically off-putting comments. Leonard has not had a good history with his girlfriends' fathers. The last told him he had a decrepit will, and when he'd first met Mr. Pajak, he had taken Leonard out onto their cabin's veranda and straight away asked him what he expected to do with the rest of his life.

Melinda answered for him, explaining how he wanted to be a human rights lawyer at the international level and try despotic criminals.

"Lovely," said Mrs. Pajak.

Mr. Pajak frowned. "What would you consider the greatest event in the history of civilization?"

"*Umm*," said Leonard, "the invention of penicillin?"

"Nope," said Mr. Pajak happily.

Leonard frowned and vowed to succeed with his dreams at all costs. He fantasized about eventually graduating from law school at Yale and stuffing his diploma in Mr. Pajak's face while telling him he now works for the United Nations so eat it.

"Oh, *stop*," said Mrs. Pajak. "I'm sure Leonard wants to relax and enjoy his weekend away from camp."

"If I were, for instance, the director of your camp," said Mr. Pajak. "I would abolish religion and teach the children to think for themselves."

"*Dad*!" exclaimed Melinda.

"Without recourse to artificial, imposed boundaries," he continued.

Afterwards, Melinda apologized profusely. She knew that Leonard was religious because it was the reason they had yet to have sex. Leonard told her that while he loved her like no other girl he had ever met, it was so written that pre-marital sex was a sin in the eyes of God.

"But only a small sin, right?" Melinda had asked, her arms taut around the length of his back, her lips tucked against his chin.

From such a position the offence seemed infinitesimal, but Leonard knew that if God did exist it was written that all sins were the same to the Lord. And Melinda had already had sex with two different boys, so he knew that if he had sex with her God would probably smite him with a sexually transmitted disease like herpes simplex or the human papilloma virus. And then Leonard's life would be ruined because when he and his future wife were having a picnic in the pristine wilderness and she wanted to have sex on a blanket in a field, he would have to tell her that he had big warts on his penis and so instead they would just have to hold hands.

Back on the course, Mr. Pajak has begun to shoot well. He birdies the seventh and eighth holes and plays the rest solidly, so that at the fourteenth he is neck and neck with Leonard and Melinda for the lead.

"I think," says Mr. Pajak. "That I am peaking at just the right time. Yes?"

"Fine," says Melinda.

"It is like I am a train and I am gathering speed as the operators fill me with coal as I come out beyond the crest of the forest and slash through the middle of the mountains."

He lines up to putt, and his ball rolls through a hoop, up a ramp, around a corner and off a sideboard just short of the hole.

"This will be another birdie," says Mr. Pajak.

"*We see*," says their mother.

"Birdies sound like this in the trees," he continues, and begins to whistle.

Melinda rises to the challenge, putting her ball directly beside their father's, deflating his celebrations.

Nelson and Mrs. Pajak both putt their own shots too far.

"Leonard, do not make any mistakes now," says Mr. Pajak. "You do not want to fall behind."

Leonard eases into a practice stroke.

"Imagine the shame of losing to me," says Mr. Pajak. "Who only just took golf up three years ago, in the minimal time I have to spare."

"*Dad*!"

"*And* I am much older than you. You have the advantage of youth."

Nelson frowns, and Leonard thankfully considers how the young boy will be different from his father. At fifteen, one year younger than Leonard and the same age as Nick, Nelson is always polite and courteous. He has the same dark eyes as his mother and sister, as well as their tanned complexion and smooth skin… Leonard breaks off the train of thought too late and has already imagined what it would feel like to grip Nelson's bum and rub his chest up against his back.

Leonard taps twice on his head and putts in distraction. It is far too slow and doesn't make it around the corner.

"Unlucky!" Mr. Pajak calls, happily swinging his club in a circle. He eases into his stance and sinks his putt: "Another successful stage in my comeback attempt."

Melinda and her mother also finish on their second shot. Only the two boys remain, and Leonard examines the green so as to avoid the thoughts catalyzed by Nelson's body.

"Your go," offers Nelson.

"He *is* furthest away," adds Mr. Pajak.

Leonard lines up his putt, seeing nothing but Nelson.

THAT NIGHT, LEONARD DOES NOT GET an attempt to make out with Melinda and prove he is straight because her father takes them out for ice cream and boasts about his victory until it is time to drop Leonard off at home. So during the week Leonard calls Melinda and asks her if she wants to go see the Christian group playing at the church near his family's cottage.

"Sure!" Melinda says, and Leonard says that they will be doing gospels—*Christian* gospels—but Melinda says she doesn't care because she just wants to see him.

On the way out that night Leonard thinks about what a wonderful girlfriend he has, that will go see a show with him even though they sing about Jesus when she doesn't even believe in him as anything more than a historical figure. He thinks that this is one more reason it is important not to be gay, because it would be horrible for Melinda to have to stop loving him. Also, she might worry that she turned him gay, and feel guilt for deteriorating Leonard's quality of life because he wouldn't be able to get married or adopt children.

Leonard's church is known for its hospitality and often gets travelling Christian acts at night, like female songwriters who sing about being touched by the Holy Spirit and travelling choirs from North Battleford and Saskatoon. Tonight's group is a barbershop quartet all the way from Montana, and they hush the room with a rendition of Psalm 23. When they finish you can hear the stained glass shifting in a draft before everyone bursts into applause. Melinda grasps his elbow so that he's white to the skin and whispers, "They're fantastic!" and Leonard agrees that there is power there regardless of whether you believe in Jesus or not.

He watches the groups' tenor, the youngest of the four, a tall, thin man smiling with abandon through a large oval mouth from under the lights. When the group launches into "All Who Are Thirsty" Leonard does not hear the words and everything around him loses shape because he has just thought that the man has a good mouth for sucking a penis.

Melinda puts her head into the crook of Leonard's shoulder. Leonard pretends to look at the stage but really looks beyond the singers to the cross in the background. *The cross is a big penis*, Leonard thinks, shutting his eyes because it is one thing to be gay and another to be blasphemous and yet another to be both together, *so the cross is not a big penis, Satan is a penis*, but soon the thoughts are escalating and he must escape outside.

Leonard treads out along the beach, feeling nothing of the night air and thinking only that he will soon have to go to a Christian camp like "Love in Action" or "Exodus," which work to repress homosexuality so that you never commit sodomy, which is second only to bestiality as the worst sexual sin. And amidst all this it occurs to Leonard that in actuality he isn't even gay. That if he were put on a desert island with just Melinda and Adam Wilson and it was just him making the decision and not his thoughts, he would choose to sleep with Melinda because she was far more attractive to him.

What Leonard needs is to discover a state of being in which everything that exists is eradicated. He wants to be newborn without experience or perception, long before his memories have so subtly shifted his preferences in one direction or another, and look up to find nothing looking back. To know what imprints his hands might make in a vacuum, the shape of his footsteps across a void. Because now there are only thoughts that he cannot control, and the only people he has heard of that cannot control their thoughts are murderers and rapists and people who get drunk and run their cars into buildings or reach out and grab women's breasts without asking.

So Leonard looks out at the moon across the lake thinking he might as well row a boat to the middle of it and throw himself overboard, if it weren't for the fact that if God exists he would smite him and send him to hell for committing suicide. Plus, his life can still have meaning in other non-sexual ways, like as a volunteer for Big Brothers or as an important politician like Pierre Trudeau, so he must save Melinda from his homosexuality and move on with these other aspects of his life.

Leonard takes a last long look back at the chapel. He will leave her there. And when she comes to call at camp he will send her excuses through little children who will confuse her and send her away. And if she waits in the parking lot he will take the back roads, and if she comes by boat he will take the highway, and if she comes to their home in the middle of the night he will tell his parents that she is addicted to drugs.

That night Leonard takes the memories of Melinda down to the floating dock. He casts them all into the lake: a bracelet, a stuffed animal, two picture books and a VHS copy of *Beverly Hills Ninja*, starring Chris Farley. And this is the manner in which love ends.

Part Four

LEONARD'S FATHER IS VERY EXCITED TO DRIVE Leonard out to the University of Victoria to begin his post-secondary education. They leave early in the morning with Nick in the back of the van, who's coming along in order to scout university locations for when his last season with the Wheat Kings wraps up in two more years.

A day later, they arrive at Leonard's new campus. They find his building and follow a rusted stairwell up ruined stairs and cross the drab shag carpet into his room.

"It's nice," says their father. "Rustic."

They stack Leonard's possessions to one side and note the non-fiction work, *Cults that Kill*, open on his new roommate's bed. There's a poster above his desk of a band called Kevorkian Death Match, with a picture of an ailing foetus wrapped in barbed wire.

"Probably metaphorical," muses Leonard's father.

Nick says Leonard's new roommate looks like he sucks and that they should all wait to meet him together and lay down the law, but their father insists that they stop in at their Aunt Mona's for dinner. They drive back across town with both Leonard and Nick lamenting the meeting, each for their own reason, although only Nick is vocal about it.

"I don't like Aunt Mona," he says morosely.

Their father turns around, injured. "She's your mother's sister!"

But Nick says she reminds him of a math teacher he once had that ended all of her sentences with "*tres bon.*"

"Well that's hardly her fault," explains their father. "What about Geoff and Talia—you like them."

"Because they can't talk."

"Well they can now," says their father. "Geoff's almost seven. He's quite the little conversationalist. You can talk to him about the U.S. Open."

Leonard cringes at the idea of spending the evening with his two little cousins, as children are the subjects of his latest thoughts. At the end of this last summer at Camp Duchesne, Nick had told him a story about a hockey coach who had been arrested after he was discovered in the shower room with lubricant, bondage tape and one of his younger players. Leonard's stomach had rolled at the thought of it, but that night the thought came to him that he might also want to rape children, and then the walls came down around him and when he arose the next morning he closed his eyes on his campers and scrambled into the forest.

For the remainder of the camp, he brushed his teeth outside the bathroom and retired from any sporting activities that might require contact with his campers. At night, he tapped his head until the skin bruised below his cowlick, and ran visions of them in all sorts of compromising positions back and forth through his mind in order to ensure that he did not want to rape them, *no matter what, ever*, but it never did any good. Even if these thoughts turned out to be false, there was no guarantee they would not come the next time he was doing something pleasurable, like eating a banana or making love to a woman or hearing a brilliant song on the radio, and perhaps these two experiences would coincide, so then he will have been sexually excited by children, which was the most abhorrent act in the world.

Leonard considers the clean mantles of his childhood home and the clear glass windows from which he could view the calm and quiet of his residential street. He was not raised to be a monster. And yet now when he looks in the mirror he is examining the face of a pedophile, even though *he did not want to do it, did not, not*. But the thought was there within him, like any other thought, like hating a movie or liking pickles or disagreeing with a point in History class, and if he was responsible for one idea he was responsible for them all. And so he would be put in prison and raped because everyone hates child molesters, even their fellow criminals, and the guards just watch as pedophiles get fucked in the ass because they are only getting what they deserve.

WHEN THE FAMILY ARRIVES AT THEIR AUNT'S they are immediately ushered out of the house. Aunt Mona apologizes profusely for the inconvenience, but their meal has gone awry.

"I'm so sorry, Doug," she says. "I had the whole chicken ready to go, but my mind was elsewhere. Talia was screaming in the back about something—I put salt in the sauce and covered the entire thing. I was making that sweet and sour sauce, with the pineapple glaze. I thought it was the sugar. Oh, it's ruined!"

Their father explains that that is what the van is for, and the entire extended family packs in and drives eight blocks to the nearest Italian restaurant.

Leonard sits alone in the back of the vehicle to avoid touching either Geoff or Talia. Nick, flanked by both cousins, whispers to Leonard conspiratorially over the crest of the middle seat.

"I know a chicken when I smell one. There was no chicken in that house."

"We were only in the hall," whispers Leonard, not daring to look anywhere but out the window.

Out of the corner of his eye, he makes out Nick's rapid gestures towards his nose. "The smell. It *wafts*. Who are you talking to? I bet she's going to make Dad pay, too."

"What are you talking about?" Geoff asks Nick.

"There was NO chicken," Nick continues to Leonard, and then, turning to Geoff: "A secret."

"What is it?"

"That cheese is the best."

"You told me your secret!"

"Fine, but you can't tell anyone else. Now you're my double agent. Okay?"

"What's a double agent?"

"It's like a ninja," says Nick.

Geoff says he wants to be a ninja, and so Nick leans over to whisper a secret ninja code into his ear. Leonard catches the outline of the whole scenario and closes his eyes so that he does not imagine sticking his penis into Geoff's mouth because he doesn't want to do that, *he doesn't, he doesn't, no*...and then they arrive at the restaurant.

Over dinner Aunt Mona asks Nick what he wants to be when he grows up.

"A French Canadian."

"Oh, smart ass, why is that?"

"He wants to be a marine biologist, actually," says their father. "Unless he makes the NHL."

"Still a chance of that?" asks their aunt.

"The injury set him back a bit," their father explains, "but his save percentage was getting up there near the end of the year. Wasn't it, Nick?"

Nick knows he will not make the NHL and it affects him like nothing Leonard has ever seen before. He cannot look up from his plate setting for fear of looking at the kids but he knows Nick is currently biting his bottom lip and considering which epithet might be most offensive. Leonard steps in to save him.

"0.865," says Leonard. "With a goals against average of 2.21."

"Look at the brotherly love," says their aunt.

"Nick is an outstanding goaltender," says their father.

"That's the position Geoff likes," says their aunt. "Isn't that right?"

"Right!" says Geoff.

"So maybe you can get some tips from your cousin about how to be a good goalie."

"Wear large pads," mutters Nick.

Leonard's father sees the direction the conversation is headed and tries to intervene. "I see Talia is wearing some nice bracelets. Isn't she, Leonard?"

"Show your bracelets to Leonard," her mother encourages her.

Contrary to what their father has told them, Talia can only speak in coos and the odd broken word. But she understands her mother's directive and leans a shaking arm out towards him.

"Fantastic," says Leonard, still examining his place setting.

He catches his aunt frowning briefly, and Leonard realizes that she must consider him and his brother a pair of rather maladjusted young men.

"Geoff likes basketball as well," she tries again.

"But what he really wants to be is a ninja," cuts in Nick.

"Is that right?" asks Leonard's father.

"No," says Aunt Mona.

"Yes!" yells Geoff.

Nick turns to Aunt Mona. "Navy Seals practice drowning calmly so that if they are ever discovered in enemy territory they don't reveal their squad's position. That kind of discipline has to be drilled into them early."

"*Right,*" says Aunt Mona. "Thank you."

"So you have to get him scuba diving right away. Also, heavy artillery training and parachute lessons."

Their aunt slaps their father's arm when she sees him nodding his head. "I did not give up my practice to raise government-trained assassins," she says.

Nick shrugs. "Kids love the water."

"What's an assassin?" asks Geoff.

"A killer!" says Nick.

"Weren't you a camp counsellor?" asks Aunt Mona, briskly.

Leonard's father changes tack. "So, Geoff, how's your new school?"

"Last class, I got ten!"

"Wow! *Ten*! High five!"

Leonard's father leans across to give Geoff a high five, then moves across to offer the same to Leonard. This forces Leonard to spin in turn and do the same with Geoff, which results in him thinking about what his little cousin's hand would feel like on his penis. And then Leonard worries, as he always does, that Geoff can somehow sense these thoughts. And so now Geoff is ruined forever, even though he is still so young and bright and getting ten in one of his classes, he will always be mixed up in the head because he now knows he's been the victim of sexual abuse.

The table descends into silence a moment after the food arrives. Aunt Mona has ordered chicken, which has been gnawing away at Nick for some time now.

"You sure must love chicken," he says.

"It's fine," she responds.

"Well, you've been cooking it all day," says Nick. "I thought you might be sick of it by now."

Aunt Mona licks the meat off a bone. "It doesn't take all day to cook chicken."

"Really?" asks Nick, with feigned shock. "Then how long does it take?"

"Less than an hour."

"Nick's a great cook," says their father. "He's cooked some really great chicken. You guys should swap recipes."

"Then how come he doesn't know how long it takes to cook it?" asks Aunt Mona.

"He means the sauce. Don't you, Nick?"

Nick ponders a moment. "I do," he says at last. "I *do*."

"The sauce takes longer," says his aunt.

"Really?" asks Nick. "How much longer?"

"A few hours."

"A *few*." Nick turns to Geoff. "Was your mother cooking for *a few* hours today?"

"No!" says Geoff.

"Really? What was she doing?"

"Fixing her hair," says Geoff.

"*Fixing her hair*!" says Nick.

"That's right," says their aunt breezily. "How do you like it?"

"It looks great!" says their father.

"How did you have time to do that and cook the chicken?" asks Nick.

"I'm a miracle woman."

Nick simmers a moment in frustration. "What's in your sweet and sour chicken?" he asks finally.

Aunt Mona measures him. "Ginger."

"Is that all?"

"Cloves, honey." She pauses. "*Pineapples.*"

Their father is quick to finish his plate and request the bill. After he has finished signing for it, Aunt Mona looks over.

"Oh, here, let me get that," she says.

"Forget it," says their father.

"But you're *company*!"

"Forget it—you get the next one."

"Well, you hardly come out to visit."

"Take Leonard out some time," says his father. "He'll need a home-cooked meal."

"Perhaps your sweet and sour chicken," says Nick, quite pleased with himself.

In the parking lot, Nick puts his arm around Geoff in victory and asks him who would win in a fight between a policeman and a fireman if neither were allowed steroids. Geoff asks what steroids are, and Leonard looks on in curious fascination, amazed at how Nick touches Geoff without repulsion, as though it were any other event in the day.

AFTER HIS FAMILY RETURNS TO CALGARY, Leonard can no longer sleep nights for fear that he is a pedophile. At first, he offers prayers of forgiveness to the Lord, but soon there is no time amidst the images of little boys getting bent over his penis and little girls going down on him in their skirts. In the attempt to catch himself feeling attracted, he focusses on the details: the boys' fair hair and pale white skin, the girls' trim legs and budding breasts. And whether he thinks he has caught himself or is certain he is repulsed, he must always check again—always, just once more to be sure, until he is crying softly under his new roommate's snores.

The first friend Leonard makes in university is a hippy named Sean, who plays the djembe in a tree outside their window for three hours a day while wearing a colossal dashiki that swallows his bones like a sausage over a toothpick. Leonard's roommate says Sean has no rhythm and wishes he would shut the fuck up, but Leonard runs into him in the dorm washroom one night and Sean talks to him for an hour and a half about the dangers facing the planet and what can be done to preserve the world's natural environment for generations to come. In return, Leonard lies and tells Sean that his parents' Vietnamese foster kid, Hoai, is actually his own and that they are in regular correspondence.

"Excellent," Sean says. "A truly global exchange. You should come to my next environmental club meeting."

The next day, Sean introduces Leonard to his circle of friends that smoke reefer out by the school fountain. Leonard declines the marijuana because he understands it robs you of your ambitions and makes you want to stare at the muscles on your forearm all day, while the group gets so stoned they wander aimlessly into the library and get lost on the second floor.

"Look how many pages are in this thing," one of them says, handing his friend an encyclopedia, and stressed-out Math students threaten them with rulers.

Sean is a vegetarian and tells Leonard that he shouldn't eat the cheeseburgers or shepherd's pie from the cafeteria because they come from slaughtered cows that have been hung by their necks and prodded up the ass with electric rods.

"Big fuckin' whoop," say some nearby jocks, and they all order roast beef.

"What about the chicken?" Leonard asks, but Sean tells him that is also no good because their beaks are cut off while they're alive and they're stuffed with hormones and crammed into holding pens so that they end up pecking each other to death.

Leonard settles on a bowl of Jell-O, but Sean says that gelatin is made with horse hooves.

"Horse hooves are delicious," a young woman sitting across from them interrupts, and spoons some of it into her mouth.

Sean is so crippled by her beauty it takes him a moment before his principles get the better of him.

"To be more specific," he expands, "it is created by the prolonged boiling of animal skin, connective tissue or bone."

"*Perhaps*," the young girl says, and suddenly Leonard no longer cares about horse hooves. That night, he goes back to the cafeteria and shovels pork into his mouth because sin is relative and if he is already a pedophile who is currently thinking about a child getting fucked on a seesaw then there is no point to saving something as inconsequential as a pig. There is no point to doing anything, not even believing in God, because even the most fervent worship would never save you if you tried to get through the gates of heaven after molesting a child. Leonard thinks, in fact, it is actually worse to feign compassion because then at his pedophilia trial Sean will take the stand and make an impassioned case for how Leonard wanted to save orphans in Vietnam and boycott factory farming, and it will all seem like a big front. The prosecuting attorney will have a field day with it, and after Leonard dies and is judged by the Lord the angels will wag an extra finger at him for not only being a pedophile but a hypocrite as well.

Leonard spends every night in his room, trying to steel himself against the terror by tapping himself twice on the penis for every horrible thought. He misses out on important social events, like the time the boys from his building got so drunk they rounded up some of the campus rabbits and put them in the girls' bathrooms. At first, everything went well because soon there were clusters of girls in housecoats who'd been scared out of their showers running after any boy wielding a carrot. The girls shook their curling irons at them and lashed at their ankles with the electric cords.

"It was awesome," Leonard hears them say afterward. "We got whipped!"

But then someone had called Emergency and the

girls stopped chasing them around in their nighties and started talking to the firemen instead, and Jessica Swan even got a date with one of them.

"Which one?"

"The guy holding the hose."

"It's *always* the guy holding the hose!"

The one social event Leonard does attend is the Halloween dance, after he and Sean get so drunk he can't focus on his ruminations. The girl who likes Jell-O is there, dressed as Marilyn Monroe, and after speaking to her for fifteen minutes Leonard throws his mouth on her chin and starts muttering incoherencies about loneliness and desperation.

The next morning Leonard wakes up to the powdered smell of an unfamiliar bed and the sound of the girl's mouth on his body. For a moment, there is only the thin line of her lips and the peaceful dash of an eyelash across his waist, but then the ceiling starts to lower onto his forehead as he thinks that he doesn't dare orgasm—what if he produces more cum than normal or the orgasm is extra fierce, then this could be taken as a result of his thoughts about child molestation. And, yes, he has to orgasm sometime, even if it's in his sleep, and if it's in his sleep it might as well be with a beautiful woman because what's the difference—but the difference he knows is the intention, and the only thing worse than being a pedophile is being a pedophile on purpose.

But he and the girl have already gained so much speed it is like a train putting on the brakes. Leonard attempts to focus on the normal, surrounding details to make himself pure—her legs like beanstalks beneath him, the fine arch of her eyebrow, her soft breath into the lilac of her sheets. But Leonard's thoughts have encompassed him everywhere for the past few weeks, they have shrouded him so that even if this moment were as holy as the hills of Nazareth, surely at least one of the thoughts about child molestation could be said to have added to his pleasure, so he cannot go through with this, *never*—and then it is suddenly happening, without his consent, and for a moment everything is lost to him.

And when the feeling of doom disappears as he ejaculates and descends again as he finishes, he hardly reacts. Leonard realizes how habituated he is to terror, how he knows it the same way he knows consciousness, how the two are inexorably married in the same fluid manner as thought and action. He looks down at the girl knowing they are damned, and there is a certain calm to everything, as though he really were evil and at peace with his transgressions, so that before he leaves the room he very nearly drops off to sleep.

＞￢＼￢＜

RIGHT BEFORE HE IS TO RETURN HOME to Calgary for Christmas, Leonard commits theft for the first time and steals sutures from an unmanned supply room at the university health clinic.

When Leonard arrives home, his brothers are already there.

"I'm going to put on three thousand pounds starting right now," says Nick, and sits down in front of one of his mother's enormous sandwiches.

Fifteen minutes later, the family piles into the car to go out for supper.

"I'm starving!" says Nick.

Their father is so excited to have everyone back he peels out of the driveway and the flag on their mailbox falls from the breeze.

"Be careful," says their mother.

"I'm the best driver in the world," says their father.

"Last time we hit a bird," she tells the kids.

"We didn't *hit* it," their father responds.

"No?"

"I would say *grazed.*"

"I didn't know you hit a bird," says Steve.

"Your *father* did," says their mother.

"Grazed," says their father.

"Well, did you go back for it?" asks Steve.

"It was fine," says their father.

"What would they have done with it?" Leonard asks Steve.

"Take it to the SPCA!"

But Nick says that the SPCA wouldn't do anything because they have thousands of stray dogs and cats to look after every hour, so what would they care about one little bird that was probably too dead to recover?

"They have procedures in place," says Steve.

"Birds are good at dodging cars," replies Nick. "The one they hit was probably demented anyways."

"*Grazed*," says their father.

"You're saying it was suicidal?" asks Steve.

"Either that or it just sucks at being a bird," says Nick. "Surfing on air currents is their thing."

Steve says that is ridiculous but either way they should have gone back because otherwise they're just being speciesist. "If it was, say, a little kid, they would have gone back to check on it!"

"*Because* it's a little kid," says Nick.

Steve says that we're all living beings and to make distinctions between children and animals is entirely random because the only real difference between the two is a capacity for language. "And while you wouldn't kill a differently abled child, who also has no capacity for language, I bet you wouldn't think twice about killing a gorilla."

"Who's killing a gorilla?" Nick asks.

"People do it all the time!"

"I've never even *seen* a gorilla," says Nick, "and if I did I wouldn't kill it at all. I'd give it a high five for being awesome."

"That's the spirit!" says their father.

Nick says the only time he's ever heard of people killing gorillas was in that movie they had to watch in high school, *Gorillas in the Mist*, which sucked so bad he skipped all the classes.

"You skipped your classes?!" says their mother.

"Just kidding!" says Nick.

When they arrive at the restaurant, Nick is so buoyed by the thought of eating that he puts Leonard in a headlock and tells him to smell his armpit because it is the scent of pure awesome. Leonard feels himself in tight on Nick's skin, up close to a man for the first time in months, and tries to ascertain whether he is sexually attracted by all this aggression. He remembers all the times he and Nick had played basketball together, how their chests rubbed against one another's and how their bums had made incidental contact, so that maybe all along he had been attracted to his brother and wanted to molest him when he was younger.

Leonard punches Nick with all his might to get him away. To get Leonard in trouble, Nick buckles in front of their mother and tells her Leonard just broke his stomach.

"*Stop*, you two."

Inside, Nick says the restaurant is upper class so he's going to have to order two entrees. "At these places they serve those fake plate-bowls that are big around the side but don't actually hold much in the middle."

"Why don't you order *one* first," suggests their mother. "And see how you feel."

Nick grumbles into a glass of water and says that in that case he's going to have to have a steak.

Leonard sits and tries to remember every possible moment he and Nick had ever spent together naked. But there are too many to count, including some that probably went back to the time before Leonard had memory, so maybe back then he had reached over and grabbed Nick's penis. And maybe this had led to the self-esteem problem that Steve always diagnosed Nick with, so now Leonard will never be able to hug his brother again because then his penis will stick against Nick's thigh and Leonard might get excited, and this would be like molesting Nick all over again and just make things worse.

Leonard feels the urge to cleanse himself, and so he excuses himself to go to the washroom. He enters the stall and brings his pants down, going green at the sight of what he has already done to himself, but takes himself in hand nonetheless. He aims at the black sore and brings his fist down as hard as he can.

Leonard loses sight of the lime green of the linoleum floor as his knees give. His forehead searches for the cool body of the stall, and he rests a moment, trying to convince himself that one hit will be plenty. Otherwise he might not make it back to dinner and his secret will be bared for the entire family, but two is what he always promises himself, and for being weak and arguing he will now make it three. He staggers up to punch himself again, the clean porcelain of the toilet wavering and then settling once more into vivid reality as the pain bursts forwards in a spasm that extinguishes all other sensations as he rides it out through oblivion and the heavy throbbing sets in. Again, he thinks that he should stop, but if he argues any longer he will make it four hits on himself, so instead he tries to stand, but he has fallen down on the toilet and his legs won't move.

Leonard tells himself that if he does not get up in five seconds he will hit himself a dozen times. This brings enough adrenaline to project himself to his feet. And before he brings his hand down a third time he thinks that he is in the midst of proving that he can motivate himself to do anything, and this is a good lesson to bear in mind because one day this means he will be cured of all evil through sheer force of will. But then his hand comes down and the intensity is upon him once more, and it is like a dream where he only has a handle, and not a certain lock, on everything around him.

IT IS NOT THAT DIFFICULT TO CUT your own testicles off. Before he shot Abraham Lincoln's assassin, Boston Corbett was worried about having sex with prostitutes and so he just took a pair of scissors and lopped them off and afterwards he went to a prayer meeting and sat down for a meal. And there was once a man working at a mill in Pennsylvania who got himself caught in the machinery and accidentally sliced through his scrotum, but was so embarrassed he stapled it together and just went back to work.

Leonard knows this because he has been doing extensive Internet searches for over two months. The day after the idea had come to him he sat down at the computer in the school library and typed "how to cut your balls off" into the Google search engine. He examined the screen with his head up close to it and both hands on either side of his temples in order to shield it from passers-by, because there were strict rules against pornography on school computers, and while he was unsure if giant hi-resolution images of mutilated

genitals were considered pornography, in any case he
didn't want to be caught looking.

Leonard spent hours pouring over first-hand do-it-
yourself accounts of those who had been brave enough
to extricate themselves from predicaments of gender
identity disorder and pedophilia. He feels at one with
them, and even though he cringes because they are
locked up in prisons and insane asylums and spurned
by humanity, he knows that if he takes matters into his
own hands quickly enough he can live a fairly productive life as a bachelor interested in solitary activities. At
the very least, it would make certain that he never hurts
anyone, so at the end of his life during the eulogy the
worst that could be said was that he was boring, but
never that he was a monster.

Yet Leonard is uncomfortable with the pressure of
performing his own surgery in order to ensure that
his scrotum doesn't go black and swell to the size of
a coffee pot from excessive bleeding, which seems to
happen quite often. Even though the procedure seems
quite simple and only requires Lidocain, a hemostat,
an exacto knife, antiseptic, needles and sutures, when
Leonard thinks back to junior high he remembers how
he couldn't even drill proper axle holes in the wood
block for his CO_2 car, so therefore cutting a one-inch
incision in his scrotum might be a bit beyond him. But
everyone unanimously agrees that once the testicles are
gone the children are definitely left alone, and if this is
the foundation on which good rests, then it has to be
done.

On Boxing Day, Leonard borrows his parents' car on the pretence of going to play basketball and takes the highway straight south out of the suburbs to the prairie farmland shrouded in ice awaiting the thaw. The town of Nanton holds a few thousand and runs two main streets parallel to the highway. The veterinarian is just on the cusp of the main village, but Leonard parks his father's car three blocks away so that the staff members don't see him drive up in a Passat.

Leonard is dressed in cowboy garb he found in the basement from the time Steve acted in a high school western. Steve had sat around in the clothes for two days trying to get his accent correct, and Nick had snuck up to the door to capture the attempts for posterity on their father's voice recorder. But after Nick realized he'd taped over an entire week of his father's personal reminders, he erased all the evidence and re-recorded over Steve with silence. Their father missed three appointments and told their mother he was getting Alzheimer's.

As Leonard steps into the veterinarian clinic, he wonders if his father's chuck wagon belt buckle isn't overdoing it. But he has to pretend that he's getting Lidocaine in order to castrate a horse, so he can't exactly look like he's taking General Studies at the University of Victoria.

The vets hand over the drug just like that, and Leonard tips his hat to highlight his wide-eyed innocence and show that there was no way he would use these supplies on himself to cut his own testicles off.

On the way home Leonard stops at the pharmacy for antiseptic and drives to the outskirts of the downtown core to buy a hemostat and a pocket knife at a uniform store. But Leonard is shocked to find the store closed, which is ridiculous because its Boxing Day, the life and breath of the consumer industry, and people closed on this day should not be allowed to operate in the capitalist system because sheer traffic volume alone would probably increase their revenue by at least twenty-five percent, and Leonard should know because he just took first year Micro Economics.

Leonard paces around outside the store, intent on buying a lifetime supply of hemostats from a competing company just to show his respect for good business sense, when he spots a window inches open above the back door. He jumps onto a garbage bin below it and pulls himself through, landing inside with the sudden thought that the owners of the uniform store might have a silent internal alarm that sends a dispatch to the police. And then he worries that he broke into the store because he wanted to get caught and put in prison so that he won't have to go through with the castration. So to prove himself wrong, he hides his face from any potential security cameras by bringing his sweater up over his head. He moves quickly about the store with only his eyeballs showing, finds the items he is looking for, and tears back to the window. He kicks off the wall in an attempt to propel himself upwards, but he misses the window by a good foot and the sweater comes off his face. He lands awkwardly on his cowboy boots and rolls his ankle.

And now the security cameras would have spotted him for sure, so he tries the jump again, this time with the sweater down around his neck so that he can swing his arms. He misses again and his ankle burns in pain, and he thinks that he will now be trapped in here until the store's staff members show up the next morning. And what kind of Christmas will Leonard have given his family, what with a botched break and enter on an easy score that had no alarm system and an open window, on Boxing Day, all to get a hemostat and a pocket knife to cut his balls off.

Leonard concocts a Plan B, which involves waiting for the store staff to enter through the back door the next morning and then rushing them with a big box in his hands and the sweater over his head screaming *"Ahhhhh!!!"* so that they get distracted and he can get away. But that involves waiting for almost twenty-four hours, and meanwhile his father's car will get towed and a security company might find him on a routine check and call the police. And judging by what he's stolen the cops will know he wants to cut his balls off because he's a child molester, and then they'll search his record for prior convictions and interview his whole family. Nick will find out that Leonard's been wanting to molest him since he was five, and when he gets out on bail Nick will be waiting there with a baseball bat to tattoo the underside of his eyes.

But eventually Leonard remembers the front door. He opens it and slides safely out into the street, feeling guilty for leaving the store unlocked behind him, though this is what happens when you close your store on Boxing Day and have no respect for the free market economy.

Leonard reaches his car and sits in the front seat with the hemostat and knife laid out beside him. Then he makes his way through the late morning traffic back home.

THAT NIGHT, THE FAMILY HAS ITS LAST dinner of the season together. According to custom, they go around the table and talk about what they have achieved that year and what they hope to accomplish in the next.

When it's Leonard's turn he thinks of what it would be like to tell everyone that this year he pretty much became a child molester and threw his soul away into the bowels of hell. And what he wants for next year is one of those country doctors he reads so much about on the Internet, who perform castrations for a couple of hundred dollars under the table. You take a week off work and show up the night before and stay at a bed and breakfast down the street. The next morning, you take a slow gravel road two minutes to the doctor's door and sit in the cool immaculate blue of his operating room and watch his poised, precise instruments standing by. And he puts you under full of ugliness, but when you come back there's nothing to consider but the dull pain in a clear head. And then you spend three more days down the road, eating breakfast with a proprietor who wears large plaid dresses and talks fondly of a husband who died in the war. You go back to the doctor once a day for check-ups but everything is on course, and now when you walk at dusk to the local eatery and pull up into a booth at the back with the naugahyde seats and the flowered plastic tabletop and there's a family in front of you drinking root beer with the kids staring at you over the back of their chairs, it's okay. And you smile.

"I'm glad that things have gone well with school," says Leonard. "And for next year, I don't know. I hope Steve gets married."

><><

LEONARD RETURNS TO THE UNIVERSITY and brushes his teeth in the dormitory with all the instruments necessary to cut off his testicles tucked into his toiletries case. He goes into the bathroom stall and runs the knife's edge against the sensitive skin on the underside of his scrotum. He brings his testicles as low as possible in the sack, doubles a rubber band around them to cut off the blood supply, and imagines…but does not break the skin.

Before bed, Leonard's roommate follows the latest pedophile on the news. His three-year jail term is up, and in the little B.C. town he has recently holed up in, everyone is railing against the system and throwing bricks through his window and driving their children the one block to school. Leonard watches and wonders about this particular man on the day he had first thought of committing his atrocity. If he'd been in a coffee house, or his own home, or a Chinese restaurant with white walls on a Saturday afternoon. Whether or not he'd been in the supermarket and the thought had made him drop a grapefruit.

Leonard thinks he knows something about this man because they have contemplated the same thing. Leonard knows from his own experience that existence sometimes overrides preoccupation, because no matter how many thoughts he has, he will sometimes, in spite of everything, find himself studying for class, or worrying about the weather, or laughing at a joke.

And so it is impossible for Leonard to see this man as a monster, when he knows that in many important respects he is just like anyone else. When Leonard imagines him he thinks of a man easily recognizable in anyone—a man perusing a restaurant menu because he has food preferences, who would plead not to die, in regular contact with his mother, who might have once had a date in high school.

As his roommate turns off the lights, Leonard imagines a time when no one had yet to indecently touch a child. When everyone slept softly and they only needed blankets to protect themselves from the cold. But then it happened, and happened again, and just kept happening, at the hands of people competent enough to drive a car or sign for a business license, who got hungry at noon and fatigued after a long day, who sometimes even paid taxes and at the very least had the command of a language. People who had not yet committed the unspeakable, and, for whatever the reason, sometimes moved forward with it before first strapping themselves to a bed or tying themselves to a tree or binding themselves to a stake in the woods.

Leonard wakes up the next day and carries the requisite instruments for his own destruction around to all of his classes. During Psychology, the professor is discussing the Stockholm syndrome and a young woman stands up and announces that when she was growing up her father used to beat her mother. It was something consistent, like breakfast, but she still loves him because life isn't easy and makes no sense, and wounds leave space on the body for the heart to grow into.

After class, Leonard walks back to the cafeteria thinking that he could count on the same unconditional love from his own family. That his parents would still send him parcels in prison, that his brothers, after many years, would come around to making fun of the orange jumpsuit. They would all forgive the unforgivable, and this is why he has promised himself that if he was ever to act on a thought, he would first lunge into the nearest bathroom stall and cut himself clean. Because if sins are not premeditated, they are originally shaped as quiet, uncertain accidents, and so he is the only one able to police himself against them and hold himself accountable.

So far, Leonard has refrained from this on the chance that he is good. When he arrives back to his dormitory, he and Sean go to the cafeteria, and when they come back there are only two more hours left in the day. One more day he will have survived intact. One more day he will have kept this possibility alive: that he might soon wake up to realize that he simply has a strange way of caring about the world, and, after all, everyone is safe.

ABOUT THE AUTHOR

Photo: Randall Okita

Brendan McLeod is a writer, musician, spoken word artist and former Canadian SLAM poetry champion who has featured at hundreds of literary festivals around the world. When he's not writing or performing solo, he tours with The Fugitives, a spoken word and music collective whose live performances and two CD releases have received critical acclaim. Brendan was raised in Saskatchewan and Alberta, earned his MA in Philosophy at the University of Waterloo and now lives in Vancouver. His website is www.brendanmcleod.ca.

About the International 3-Day Novel Contest

The 3-Day Novel Contest is a literary tradition that began in a Vancouver pub in 1977, when a handful of restless writers, invoking the spirit of Kerouac, dared each other to go home and write an entire novel over the weekend. A tradition was born and today, every Labour Day Weekend, hundreds of writers from all over the world take up this notorious challenge. In the 30 years since its birth, the contest has become its own literary genre and has produced dozens of published novels, thousands of unique first drafts, and countless great ideas.

The International 3-Day Novel Contest is now an independent organization, managed by a dedicated team of volunteers in Vancouver and Toronto, but it owes its existence to the publishing houses that began and sustained it, including Arsenal Pulp Press, Anvil Press and Blue Lake Books. We at the contest also thank *Geist* magazine, for its continued support, and BookTelevision, for adding a new element to the tradition with its 3-Day Novel Contest reality TV series, which launched in 2006. We are also in great debt to our volunteer judges, who give hours and hours to reading and evaluating the hundreds of novels that arrive after Labour Day each year.

For information on entering the 3-Day Novel Contest, and for a list of past winning novels, visit us at www.3daynovel.com.